"An opposites-attract romance with plenty of laugh-out-loud humor, steamy love scenes and swoony, heartfelt romance... When I say *The Chase* has it all, I *really* mean that it has it all. It's a phenomenal reading experience." — *USA Today*

"The title says it all! Kennedy's ninth Out of Uniform installment [is] an erotically charged tale of an unconventional happily-ever-after... Kennedy fans and newcomers will relish the well-crafted plot, witty dialogue, and engaging characters" — *Publishers Weekly*, Starred Review, about *Hotter Than Ever*.

"A steamy, glitzy, and tender tale of college intrigue." — *Kirkus Reviews,* about *The Chase*

"Elle Kennedy is the queen of hate-to-love-you sexy romance!"— Vi Keeland, #1 *New York Times* bestselling author

"No one writes deliciously sexy and laugh-out-loud funny better than Elle Kennedy. I loved this book!" — *USA Today* bestselling author Nikki Sloane

"No one writes intoxicating college sports romances like Elle Kennedy, and her newest novel is unputdownable... A must-read!" — *Natasha is a Book Junkie*

OTHER TITLES BY ELLE KENNEDY

Off-Campus Series:

The Deal

The Mistake

The Score

The Goal

Briar U Series:

The Chase

The Risk

The Play

Out of Uniform Series:

Hot & Bothered

Hot & Heavy

Feeling Hot

Getting Hotter

Hotter Than Ever

As Hot As It Gets

A full list of Elle's contemporary and suspense print titles is available on her website: www.ellekennedy.com.

Bad Apple

ELLE KENNEDY

Bad Apple

Previously published as *Midnight Encounters*

Edited by Aquila Editing

Cover Art © Damonza

1

MAGGIE

"Wipe that look off your face, Mags. You'll scare the customers."

I shove a wayward strand of hair off my forehead and glance over at my coworker. "What look?"

"The I'm-having-sex-in-an-hour-so-don't-hold-me-up look." With a cheerful smile, Trisha opens the icebox under the bar counter and dumps a scoopful of ice cubes into the glass pitcher she's holding.

"Damn, and I thought my poker face was solid," I reply with a grin.

Trisha pours ice water into three tall glasses and sets them on her black tray. "Don't worry, you'll see Tony soon enough."

"Who's Tony?" Matthew, the cute, blond bartender, comes up behind us, curiosity etched into his chiseled features.

I shoot Trisha a glare, the kind that says *one word and I'll kill you*. My sex life doesn't need to be common knowledge among my coworkers. It's already bad enough that Trisha knows about it, but she got me drunk one night and pried the details out of me.

To Matthew, I say, "No one. Trisha's just screwing around."

"Whatever." He shrugs and heads for the other end of the bar.

"What part of 'don't tell anyone' didn't you understand, Trish?" I ask irritably.

The brunette gives a shrug of her own. "I don't see what the big deal is. I mean, who doesn't have a Tony in their life? Casual sex is more common than relationships these days." She grins. "Though most people usually have it more than twice a year."

I ignore the mocking remark. Trisha loves teasing me about the arrangement I have with Tony, but I suspect she doesn't fully understand just how difficult it is for me to have a normal love life.

Free time doesn't exist in my life. I spend my afternoons volunteering at a youth center and my nights serving drinks at The Olive Martini. My only two nights off are reserved for my college classes. How am I supposed to find a man who could fit into—or accept—my hectic schedule? All the guys I dated in the past got tired of seeing me only once a month.

I've been dumped a lot.

Not that I'm devastated. I mean, do I even want to be with a man who can't respect dedication and a solid work ethic? I grew up dirt poor. I struggled to make ends meet all my life, scrimped and saved until I was finally able to pay for college. In a few short months, I'm going to have a degree in social work, leave the Olive, and hopefully get a permanent—paying—position at a children's welfare agency.

So, really, I don't need a boyfriend right now. Once I finish school, sure, maybe I'll start seriously dating again. But for now, I'm perfectly happy having someone like Tony Burke in my life.

Tony is a travel writer who spends eleven and a half months out of the year roaming exotic places and writing about them. He comes back to New York two or three times a year, and I met him on one of his rare visits home when he stopped in for a drink at the Olive. We instantly hit it off. Wound up in bed the night we'd met, and our trysts are now the highlights of my year.

Tony flies into town, he calls me, we have sex. Then we both return to our busy lives, sexually sated and emotionally content, with no plans to see each other again—until the next time Tony pops up in the city.

The last time I saw him was over the holidays, and since it's already May, I was expecting him to call any day now. Like clockwork, he had. Just three hours ago, with his hotel room number and the promise of some hot, stress-busting sex.

"Make fun of me all you want, Trish, but we both know you're jealous," I say good-naturedly.

"It's true. I'd give my right arm for a Tony." She makes a face. "Instead, I have a Lou."

"Aw, be nice. Lou kisses the ground you walk on."

"Yeah, when he's not watching football. Do yourself a favor, Mags. Never date a man who'd rather watch big sweaty goons chase a ball around a field than talk to his girlfriend."

I laugh. Truthfully, I've always thought the leggy brunette could do a lot better than Lou Gertz, the high school football coach slash couch potato. But whether Trisha just has bad taste in men, or Lou's a reflection of the kind of guys swimming around in the singles pool, my friend's love life only reaffirms my belief that relationships are too much of a hassle.

"Looks like Tony has some competition," Trisha quips.

I shift my gaze and notice my pot-bellied customer waving at me from across the room. "My biggest fan awaits," I say dryly. "And by the way, he heard you snickering when he commented on my waitressing skills."

Trisha snorts. "He called you a *ballerina of the bar*. He was asking for a snicker."

"You should've kept eavesdropping. I told him waitress

training is extensive and that I had to go through four years of schooling."

As Trisha giggles, I swipe the guy's credit card through the register and wait for the printer to spit out the receipt. I tuck the bill, a pen, and some mints inside a sleeve of plastic and then check my watch.

Ten-thirty. God, when is this night going to end? Normally I don't mind my shifts at the Olive. The job pays my bills, the tips are great, and I can't say I don't have fun. The staff is like a big happy family, the customers our interesting—and often completely insane—surrogate children.

But it's Tony night, and no matter how entertaining the crowd is, sex is the only entertainment I'm looking for tonight.

2

BEN

*I*f I see one more motherfucking photographer lurking in the bushes, I'm going to lose my shit. Or worse, slam my fist into someone's jaw.

Actually, that sounds so appealing, my palms tingle at the thought. But I'm not stupid. I know exactly how pointless it would be to pick a fight. The paparazzi would jump all over the story: *Violent Movie Star Assaults Innocent Photographer!* And then my reputation will take yet another hit, my agent and publicist will freak out, and I'll be forced to make dozens of morning-talk-show appearances to explain to my fans why I knocked someone's lights out.

That's how it always goes. You decide to be an actor and you say goodbye to your privacy. Doesn't matter that half the stories the tabloids run are total bullshit. If you leave the house with a runny nose, that means you snort coke. If you have lunch with a male friend, you're gay. If you shove a photographer out of your face, you have anger problems.

I've dealt with this shit for ten years, but that doesn't mean I have to like it. And I'm pissed as fuck that the vultures followed me to Manhattan. I wish I'd found a place in Colorado or

Montana for this unwanted sabbatical. Somewhere up in the mountains, so that if the press wants to harass me they'll have to work for it. Hiking up a cliff would certainly deter at least half of those nosy bastards.

But my agent insisted I go to New York. "If you want to leave Hollywood, fine," Stu had said. "But stay in sight."

In sight is the last place I want to be, but arguing with Stu is about as effective as arguing with a toddler. Eventually they'll annoy you into giving up.

"Hey, aren't you—"

I abruptly pull the rim of my Yankees cap lower so that it shields my face, then bypass the middle-aged woman who stopped in her tracks and is standing there gawking at me. Without a backward glance, I hurry along Broadway and try to disappear in the Friday night theater crowd.

Absolutely fucking ridiculous that I have to skulk around like this, but damn it, I need some peace and quiet. I bought the penthouse on the Upper East Side and moved in last week, but has the press left me alone to settle in? No way in hell. They camp out in front of the building day and night. They pay off the cleaning staff to try to snap photos of me. They bribe the doormen to let them in.

I haven't slept in seven days. Haven't been able to leave the apartment without being barraged with questions.

Were you with Gretchen the night she died?

Did Alan know about the affair?

Did he blacklist you and that's why you left LA?

So many damn questions. I don't want to deal with them anymore. Or ever.

So I took off. Left the penthouse with a trail of paps behind me, got in my rented BMW, and managed to lose the vultures somewhere in Queens. I ditched the Beemer in the first parking lot I saw, and now I'm on foot, a man on a mission, in search of the first hotel I can find that has a big bed I can finally fall asleep on.

Satisfied that I'm rid of every photographer in a ten-mile radius, I finally come to a stop in front of the Lester Hotel. There are half a dozen luxury hotels only blocks away, but I have no intention of checking in at any of them. The Lester, a ten-story building with a bland gray exterior, is the last place the vultures would think to look.

Stepping through the revolving door, I cross the empty lobby toward the front desk, where I find a skinny guy in an ill-fitting blue blazer manning the counter.

"I need a room," I mutter, pulling my wallet from the back pocket of my faded jeans.

"Single or double bed?"

"Double."

"Kitchenette?"

"I couldn't care less, kid." I fish out a wad of bills and drop them on the splintered oak counter.

"Okay then. Fill this out, please."

I scrawl a fake name and address on the clipboard that's handed to me, then push it back at the clerk.

The guy doesn't ask for ID, or even read what I wrote on the sheet. He barely spares me a second look before giving me a key. This hotel is so outdated it doesn't even use keycards. I stare at the key, which is hanging from a red plastic keychain. Classy.

Two minutes later, I get off on the third floor and breathe in the scent of potpourri and lemon cleaner.

The hotel isn't the type of accommodation I'm used to, but for once I don't care that the carpet beneath my black boots is frayed or that the doors lining the narrow corridor are in desperate need of a fresh coat of paint.

I let myself into Room 312. I don't bother turning on the light, just let my gaze adjust to the darkness and zero in on the double bed in the center of the room. Within seconds, my boots are off. T-shirt and leather jacket are tossed on the armchair. Jeans and boxers lie on the carpet.

All I care about is sleep. No phones. No agents and managers and publicists. No reporters or photographers.

Just. Fucking. Sleep.

3

MAGGIE

My steps are unusually bouncy as I hurry down the street. Normally my feet kill after a shift at the Olive, especially on Friday nights, but the only part of my body that aches right now is the spot between my legs.

I'm going to have sex.

Hell to the yeah.

I don't care if it's pathetic. So what if my only source of sexual gratification are my infrequent hookups with Tony? Relationships require too much effort, whereas the only effort I have to make with Tony is unzipping his pants. Relationships drain you—with Tony, I'm only drained after the third or fourth orgasm.

And he never makes demands on me, monopolizes my time, or acts like being a workaholic is some horrible crime. He works as hard as I do, which officially makes him the perfect man to get involved with.

I dodge a group of teenagers loitering on the sidewalk, then wave at the hot dog vendor I pass every day on the way to work. My apartment is only a few blocks from the bar, but Tony and I avoid going there. We always meet in a hotel, where we can have fun all night long and then go our separate ways in the morning.

Another perk—not sharing an awkward breakfast together the morning after.

I reach the Lester Hotel a few minutes later. I head straight for the counter and request the key for Room 312. The clerk, a very scrawny, very bored-looking guy, replies in a monotone that the room is already occupied.

"I know. He's expecting me," I answer, my cheeks warming slightly. "There should be a spare key for me. Maggie Reilly? Do you need to see ID?"

"Nah." The guy turns around and stares at the dozens of keys hanging off the hooks on the wall, then plucks one with his long, bony fingers.

Thanking the kid, I make my way to the elevator. Tony and I have visited the Lester before, so I know my way around and find the room quickly. My breasts grow heavy as I stick the key in the lock. God, I need this. With exams coming up in a few weeks, not to mention the billiards tournament the bar is holding next month, soon I'm going to be up to my eyeballs in work.

If I want to play, tonight's it.

As I let myself into the room, I'm instantly engulfed by shadows. I blink and wait for my eyes to focus, while trying to figure out the reason for the dead silence hanging over the room. No, wait, not dead silence. My ears perk as the sound of light breathing floats from the direction of the bed.

"Oh, don't do this to me, Anthony," I chide softly, dropping my purse on the table beside me and turning to lock the door. "I see you three times a year, at least have the decency to stay awake."

No response.

A slow grin spreads over my mouth as I take another step

forward. I'm tempted to flick on the lights and maybe stomp my foot to jar Tony from his slumber, but that wouldn't be fun, would it?

Instead, I reach for the hem of my T-shirt and pull the material over my head. I unhook my lacy bra. It falls onto the carpet, followed by my short denim skirt, skimpy panties and the heels on my feet.

I shiver when the cool air meets my naked skin. Then I creep toward the edge of the bed, still grinning.

"C'mon, Tony," I murmur, "you only flew in from Aruba. Don't plead jet lag."

I'm answered by a husky male groan.

"Ah, so he's alive," I tease, reaching for the corner of the flower-patterned blanket.

With a quiet laugh, I slide under the covers and press my body against Tony's, fighting back a moan as his warm, rock-hard chest presses against my bare breasts. My nipples instantly harden, the tight buds springing against the soft feathering of hair on his glorious chest.

I swing one leg over his muscular thighs, hoping the heat from my aching pussy might jumpstart his sluggish brain into action. But he remains motionless. The room is still bathed in darkness, and though I can barely see his face, it's obvious he's in a seriously deep sleep.

"I see how it is," I grumble, starting to get annoyed. "Fine. You want me to raise you from the dead? How's this?"

I place my hand directly on his crotch, a little surprised when I don't find the cotton barrier of his briefs. Since when does Tony sleep in the buff?

Not that I mind.

As a lazy heat begins dancing through my veins, I drag my index finger along the length of his shaft. Like his chest, it's rock-hard, and...bigger? No, it can't be.

I run my finger over the tip of his cock, feel the drop of moisture there, and smile as a groan breaks through the silence. Finally. Signs of life.

His massive erection tells me he'll be getting into the swing of things soon, and I'm right. The second I squeeze his shaft, one powerful arm slides out and pulls me closer. I'm suddenly crushed in his embrace, his cock still in my hand, while a pair of warm lips seeks mine out in the darkness.

His kiss steals the breath from my lungs and makes me gasp against his hot mouth. There's nothing soft or gentle about it, just a greedy devouring, the hungry thrusts of his tongue, the sting of his teeth as he bites my lower lip.

When did Tony start kissing like this?

And why hadn't he done it sooner?

The intensity of his kisses causes me to drop my hand from his erection. All I can do is lose myself in the delicious sensations his mouth and tongue create in my body. Limbs turning to jelly. Moisture pooling between my legs. Nipples so tight it's almost painful.

A fire hotter than anything I've ever experienced sweeps over me. Crackling when he bites my lip again. Hissing when he cups a breast.

And then he slips one finger into my sopping wet pussy and I'm shocked to feel the ripples of an impending orgasm rising to the surface.

Holy shit.

I clamp my teeth down on my bottom lip, trying to stop the climax. It's too fast, too soon.

How is this possible?

I've slept with this guy dozens of times before, so why is my entire body swarming with unfamiliar sensations?

I pry open my eyelids, hoping that if our gazes lock, I might make sense of it. I squint, blinking as I search his face in the dark, and then wonder why his features look more...rugged.

My gaze drifts lower and settles on his arm—is that a tattoo? When did Tony get himself inked?

And why isn't he tanned? He just came from Aruba, so really, he should have a—

"What's the matter, sweetheart?" rasps a sleepy voice.

I bolt up as if someone just shoved a ten-thousand-volt wire up my spine.

Why don't I recognize his voice?

As a steady stream of panic rushes up my throat, I gape at the dark head beside me and repeat his question in my disorientated brain.

What's the matter?

I'm in bed with a *stranger*.

4

BEN

I wake up with a jolt, sucked out of my dream thanks to a shrill female yelp.

Christ, that dream. It rivaled the one I had back in the ninth grade, that really awesome one where I fondled Cindy Mason's Double-D's. There were no Double-D's in this one, but a pair of delectable C's, and a female body with more curves than a lush valley. A hot mouth with an eager tongue. A tight wet pussy—

"Oh my God, I'm so sorry."

The mortified voice thrusts me into a fully conscious state. As I quickly collect my bearings, I glance over and see that it was all real. There's a gorgeous redhead in bed with me, as naked as I am—and she looks horrified.

"What the fuck...?" I blink a few times and finally force my hand to reach for the lamp on the nightstand.

As a pale yellow glow falls over the hotel room, I direct my gaze to the stranger next to me. She has green eyes, really pretty green eyes, despite the fact that they're swimming with fear. Her cheeks are as red as her hair, and when I look farther south, I see a crimson flush has spread over her very perky, very bare tits.

The redhead catches me staring and lets out another yelp, quickly pulling the bedcovers up to her chin to shield her nudity. Her domination of the blanket, however, leaves me fully exposed, and I sigh when I notice I'm still rocking the boner of all boners.

What the hell is going on here? I have no clue who this chick is, only that she's the sexiest sight I've seen in a while. Along with those magnetic emerald eyes and knockout figure, she has high cheekbones, a dainty nose and a sensual mouth that's just a little bit crooked. I like it, that small imperfection. It makes her all the more...real.

I wish she'd wipe that deer-in-the-headlights expression off her flushed face, though. I'm not a serial killer, for fuck's sake. And she's in *my* bed, not the other way around.

"I'm so sorry," she says again as she edges toward the side of the bed, still clinging to the blanket. "I must be in the wrong room."

I open my mouth to answer, but for some inexplicable reason the power of speech completely eludes me. What the fuck am I supposed to say anyway? No problem, thanks for giving me this stiffy?

As I watch her stumble off the bed in her blanket-toga, my confusion gives way to suspicion. Is she really in the wrong room? Sure, the skinny dude downstairs was totally incompetent and could've screwed up with the keys, but how likely is that? A much likelier possibility would be... Damn it, is she press? Did she purposely sneak into my room and try to seduce me in hopes of getting a juicy story to sell to the tabloids?

Shit.

I scramble to cover up the goods with one of the flat pillows on the bed, then narrow my eyes as the redhead scurries around the room, collecting items of clothing.

"Who are you?" I growl. My tone means business.

She falters for a moment, a black T-shirt clutched between her fingers. "What?"

"Are you a reporter?"

"Why would I be a reporter?" She appears frazzled as she stares at the shirt in her hands and then shoots me a pleading look. "Could you...could you just close your eyes for a minute while I get dressed?"

Oh, so now she's all prim and modest? Sure hadn't been that way when she was stroking my dick.

Deciding I'm entitled to a little peek, I pretend to close my eyes while watching her through slitted eyelids. I get an out-of-focus glimpse of her hooking up her bra, and my cock twitches with disappointment when her full breasts are finally covered. Is asking her to come back to bed inappropriate?

Probably.

"Okay. I'm dressed."

Yes, she is. But the tight T-shirt and short denim skirt that does amazing things to her legs only confirms she looks just as good clothed as she did naked.

"I'm mortified," she murmurs.

Then, as if she's offering a scrap of meat to a feral lion, she steps forward and hands me the blanket.

I drape it over my lower body as she continues to ramble on. "I was supposed to meet...a guy. He said this was his room number and...I guess I got it wrong. I..." She stammers, "I don't usually break into strangers' hotel rooms, I promise. I just..." She drifts off, her cheeks growing redder by the second.

Strangers?

The word hangs in the air, bringing with it another dose of confusion. She doesn't recognize me?

She actually doesn't recognize me?

I'm not conceited enough to think that all the women on the planet know who I am, but my face has been splashed on every

Hollywood rag, every entertainment show, all over social media, for weeks now. Even the elderly couple who does my dry-cleaning have heard of me, and they haven't been to the movies since the '50s.

"I'm just going to leave now, okay?" she says. "I'm sorry. I can't apologize enough for...this. I, um, I work at a bar called The Olive Martini, near the corner of Broadway and 45th, so if you're ever in the neighborhood you can pop in and the drinks will be on the house." She sucks in a deep breath. "I know a free drink doesn't make up for...um, this, but it's all I can do."

Then she clamps her mouth shut and looks at me with wide, shameful eyes, and the humor of the situation finally settles over me. A complete stranger just slipped into my bed, kissed the hell out of me, got me harder than granite, and now she's offering me free drinks to make up for it?

Laughter lodges in my throat as I try to formulate a sentence that might make the situation seem a little less insane.

I never get the chance.

With an awkward smile and another look of terror, the redhead hurries for the door.

A flash of pink from the carpet catches my eye.

"Wait," I call as she reaches for the door handle. "You forgot your—"

She slides out and closes the door with a soft click.

"—panties," I finish.

And then I give in to the urge and start to laugh.

5

MAGGIE

I tear down the street in a full-throttled run, sucking in the night air as if an overdose of oxygen will erase the pure humiliation sticking to my throat. I glance over my shoulder, half expecting to find the sexy stranger I just mauled chasing after me. Nope. All I see is the slow rush of people flowing out of one of the theaters, chattering about the show they'd just seen.

I know the dark-haired hottie isn't in the crowd, because lethal good looks like his would be impossible to miss.

How is it possible for someone to be that attractive?

When he'd turned on the lights, I had to slam my mouth closed to avoid drooling all over the hotel room carpet. He had the kind of looks you only see on male models these days—cobalt blue eyes, straight white teeth, dimples that melt your insides. But with a bit of an edge, which was highlighted by the tattoos on his biceps and chest, and the way his scruffy brown hair curled under his ears. He had bad boy written all over him. It was hot. And tempting. And thank God I got out of there.

Who knows what I would've done if I'd stayed even a second longer.

Probably fucked his brains out.

"Excuse me, coming through," I call as I weave through the same group of teenagers I passed on the way to the hotel.

"Hey, baby, what's the rush?" one of the baggy-clothed kids asks with a laugh.

I ignore the kids and push forward, my high heels clicking against the sidewalk. People keep getting in my damn way, slowing me down. All I want is to get to my building and pretend this whole hotel fiasco hadn't happened.

Why wasn't Tony there?

The question makes me stop in my tracks. For the past five minutes I've been beating myself over the head for winding up in a stranger's room, but there's no way I got the room number wrong. I wrote it on my hand.

Furrowing my brows, I flip over my hand and stare at the three digits I scribbled on my palm. It's right there—312. The ink is starting to smear, but there's no mistaking the room number. I got it right, which means that Tony—that jerk—is to blame for this entire mess.

Why hadn't he shown up? He would've called if the plan had changed, wouldn't he?

I reach into my purse and rummage around for my phone. I pull it out, and then groan. It's still on silent. I forgot to turn the ringer back on after my shift.

Five seconds later, I access my voice mail and, sure enough, hear Tony's voice.

"Hey, Mags, it's me. Listen, I've got some bad news. We had to make an emergency landing in Tallahassee. Some freak hurricane just swept in and the airline is delaying all the flights. I won't be able to get a flight out until tomorrow morning, but we're shit out of luck, babe. I have a meeting with a publisher in the afternoon and then I'm flying out to Bora Bora at five. Looks like we'll see each other next time I'm in town. Probably the end of August. Say hi to the folks at the Olive for me."

I hang up the phone and grit my teeth. *Say hi to the folks at the Olive for me?*

Anger swirls in my stomach, but deep down I know I can't blame Tony for what happened. He doesn't control the weather or the airlines, and it's not his fault that a delay I hadn't known about sent me into bed with another man.

Hell, I have nobody to blame but myself. Why on earth didn't I turn on the light when I walked in, instead of hopping into the bed and giving a stranger a handjob?

I'm the moron, not Tony.

I take a few calming breaths. It's not a big deal, right? Just a case of mistaken identity. It's not like I'm ever going to see my blue-eyed bad boy again. Well, unless he decides to show up for that free drink I offered, but how likely is that? The man probably thinks I'm a nutcase.

Which would be a very astute assumption on his part.

Unable to stop it, a giggle tears out of my throat. It's a hysterical one, sure, but at least I'm able to find some amusement in the situation. The memory of the man's bewildered eyes as he lay on the bed with an impressive erection flashes across my brain, turning the giggle into a full-out laugh.

I resume the walk home, my humiliation fading at each click of my heels. Okay, so I molested a man whose name I don't even know. Big deal. He'd liked it. I liked it too. Nobody was harmed. And we'll probably never cross paths again, so really, what harm had been done?

By the time I reach my building, my nerves have started to calm. I use my key to get into the lobby, then step inside and greet the security guard behind the desk. Considering the building is less than a dozen blocks from Central Park, the rent should have been astronomical. When I moved here from

Albany, I thought I'd never be able to find a decent place that wouldn't drain my savings account, but on my very first day in Manhattan I hit the jackpot.

Summer Windsor, a former waitress at the Olive, was subletting an apartment owned by her grandmother, and when Summer learned I was currently living in a motel, she offered me her spare room. The rent is peanuts, which allows me to save for college, and I don't even mind sleeping on the couch whenever Summer's grandmother comes for a visit. Actually, I kind of look forward to Nana's visits. For a girl who'd grown up with zero family, sometimes it's nice having someone dote on me.

As I ride the elevator up to the tenth floor, I glance at my phone again. It's almost one a.m., which means Summer is either sleeping, staying at her boyfriend's, or practicing her steel drum.

Please don't let it be option number three.

My prayers go unanswered—when I walk into the apartment, I'm instantly met by a wave of jingly notes, my roommate's rendition of "Under the Sea".

"You're still at it, huh?" I sigh, tossing my purse on the coffee table before collapsing on the couch.

"The wedding is in three days," Summer replies from the other side of the room. "I have to practice."

She's set up the drum right in front of the small dining room window. The people who live in the building across the alley have screamed at her on numerous occasions to keep her day job. I agree with them, but I can't deny I find the whole thing kind of amusing. Summer, the blonde-haired, blue-eyed accountant, banging away on a steel drum so that she could play it at a Jamaican wedding reception.

Summer met Tygue, the man of her dreams, during a vacation to Montego Bay. The two fell head over heels for each other, and a month later Tygue moved to New York. They've been inseparable for more than a year now, and they're flying back to Jamaica in a few days to attend Tygue's brother's wedding.

Where Summer got the idea to play the steel drum for the joyous event, who the hell knows. I can't see Tygue asking his girlfriend to do it, so I'm a bit terrified that she'd come up with the idea all on her own.

"I wasn't expecting you back tonight. Why aren't you with Tony?" she says, biting her lip in concentration as she bangs away on the large instrument.

"You don't want to know," I reply with a groan. I kick off my heels and rest my legs on the glass coffee table.

My ears get a much needed reprieve when Summer stops drumming. Pale blue eyes flickering with curiosity, she rises from the stool and asks, "What happened?"

Before her butt can even land on the sofa cushion beside me, half the story has already spilled out of my mouth.

When I'm done, Summer is laughing uncontrollably.

"Yes, laugh at me," I say with a frown. "It makes me feel so much better."

"Oh God, I can't believe you did that," she blurts between giggles.

"Well, believe it. Honestly, I've never been more humiliated in my life. This even beat the time in fifth grade when that snotty Billy Turner made fun of me for being in foster care."

"Jeez, that is bad." She pauses. "Was he hot, at least?"

"Hot is an understatement. He was..." I search my vocabulary for the right adjective and come up empty-handed. "Indescribably good-looking."

Summer looks intrigued. "Nice body?"

"Oh yeah. And he had that whole rebel thing going on. Messy hair, tattoos, the I'm-too-cool-to-shave thing happening."

"Oooh, like Colin Farrell!"

"Who?"

"Your ignorance about sexy actors amazes me, Mags."

"This guy wasn't an actor. I mean, he did look vaguely familiar, or at least he does the more I picture him in my head, but I think he was just a normal dude trying to get some sleep—until I showed up and practically mauled him."

"Did he like it?"

I think about the erection I stroked, and fight back a shiver. "Oh yeah."

"Then no harm done." She shrugs. "He'll probably wake up tomorrow and think it was all a dream. He doesn't even know your name, unless you left your driver's license on the nightstand or something."

I tuck a stray hair behind my ear and feel a warm flush spread over my face. "As a matter of fact, I did leave something behind."

Summer furrows her eyebrows. "What?"

A wail slips out of my mouth before I can stop it. "My underwear."

After a moment of silence, she releases a high-pitched laugh that has me flinching. "Priceless!" she cries. "That is absolutely priceless!"

My roommate's laughter brings back the wave of embarrassment I've been trying to suppress. All I wanted to do tonight was, well, Tony. Instead, I made an idiot of myself in front of a complete stranger, and now I have to live with the knowledge that I stripped naked, hopped into bed with a guy I didn't know and stuck my tongue down his throat.

On the bright side, at least I never have to see him again.

6

BEN

I stride down East 45th Street with a cup of coffee in my hand, breathing in the early morning air. I grimace when I inhale a gust of car exhaust. I fucking hate New York. Too damn crowded, and it stinks here. Literally.

As I pause in front of a jewelry store to take a sip of my coffee, I can't help but glance at my reflection in the large window.

What I see is an unshaved jaw, circles under my eyes and a bloodshot expression, all of which confirm what I already knew —I look like shit.

It was another sleepless night for me, only this time it had nothing to do with photographers lurking outside my house and everything to do with the redheaded tornado who swirled into my room.

The more I replayed her stuttering explanation in my head, the less I believed my midnight visitor was one of the vultures. I believed it even less when I grabbed the morning paper at the kiosk across the street from the Lester and didn't see my picture on any of the tabloids on the rack.

If Red was a reporter, the story of her seduction would've at least made the Tattler, a rag known for keeping page space open for last-minute "scoops."

Since it hadn't, I suspected she'd been telling the truth, that she'd ended up in the wrong room, in bed with the wrong guy.

And just like Cinderella, Red left her prince a sweet little parting gift: a pair of pink lace panties.

And an offer of a free drink.

Under normal circumstances, I would've tossed the panties and passed on the booze, but last night had been anything but normal.

Sure, the make-out session had been hot, but what turned me on most about her was that she genuinely didn't seem to know who I was.

Everything I do is highly publicized, from my appearances at the Oscars and the Golden Globes to my hookups with a fair share of models and actresses. Whether I want them to or not, women know who I am. They gawk at me when I pass them on the street. They send me thousands of tweets, dirty DMs, and unsolicited nudes. I've been called a heartthrob and a hunk, a devil and an angel, and the last time I appeared on Jimmy Fallon I got mobbed outside the studio.

So how in fiery hell didn't she know about me?

I've spent enough years working in the film industry to know when somebody is bullshitting me, and I honestly don't think I was lied to last night. Red had been oblivious to my celebrity status, and considering she hadn't salivated at the mere sight of me, I suspect she'd be unimpressed about it anyway.

Damn but that's a huge turn-on.

I quicken my pace, my gaze darting around in search of the lot where I parked my car. I remember it was near that theater where I performed in *Hamlet* last year, and there might've been a Starbucks around too, and a—

Strip club.

I stop so abruptly I nearly fall over backwards. Oh man, oh man. All I wanted was to get the paparazzi off my back. In retrospect, I really should've studied my surroundings before ditching my car. I parked in front of a fucking strip club.

So much for avoiding scandals.

I'm startled when I notice a crowd beginning to gather at the curb. I move closer, growing more and more uneasy as I spot an army of police officers and yards of yellow crime-scene tape.

Surrounding my shiny silver Beemer.

What the fuck?

Taking a step back, I try to blend into the crowd. The BMW, I notice when I peek over a woman's head, is stripped completely. The doors are gone. The engine too, from the looks of it. It's like a pack of hyenas pounced on it sometime during the night and picked its carcass clean. That doesn't surprise me. What does is the presence of New York City's finest.

Why do the cops care about my car?

I find out soon enough, as the woman in front of me leans over and whispers something to her friend.

"It's Ben Barrett's car," she hisses.

Her friend, a chubby brunette, lets out a gasp. "The actor?"

"Yep. I heard one of the officers mention it." The woman lowers her voice to a breathy whisper. "They think he's been abducted."

What?

It takes every ounce of willpower to keep my jaw off the dirty sidewalk.

Head spinning, I edge away from the murmuring crowd and walk as casually as my legs will allow. I glance around, notice the coffee shop at the corner, and make a beeline for it.

I need to call my agent and clear up this whole ridiculous mess, a plan that becomes vital the second I enter the café and hear my name blaring from the television screen over the counter.

"Bad-boy action star Ben Barrett is believed to have been abducted," a nasal-voiced reporter is saying into her microphone. "His car was found stripped and abandoned in front of a local New York City club, and police fear the worst."

Shoving the rim of my cap as low as it will go, I pause in front of the long chrome counter and glance at the screen. I instantly swallow a groan when I notice that the female reporter is reciting her broadcast from directly in front of the Lester Hotel.

I bite back a curse when the skinny desk clerk enters the frame.

"I'm now talking to Joe Dorsey, an employee of the hotel where Ben Barrett was last seen. Derek, what can you tell us about your encounter with Barrett?"

I curl my hands into fists.

"Well, he looked very agitated," the kid says, his eyes darting from the microphone to the camera trained on him. "He looked nervous."

"What do you mean by nervous?"

"I think he was on drugs."

The reporter feigns shock.

"And he wasn't alone," the kid adds, then waves at the camera and mouths, "Hi, Mom."

"Are you saying Ben Barrett met someone here last night?"

"Not someone. A woman. She came in an hour after he did." Dorsey grins, which causes his bony face to jut out awkwardly. "I think they were engaging in sexual relations, Katie."

The blood rushing to my head prevents me from hearing the end of the interview. Fists clenched, I stalk toward the deserted corridor by the restrooms.

I fish my phone out of my back pocket and call my agent.

"Ben, are you okay?" Stu Steinberg's voice booms after we've been connected.

"I'm fine," I say with a sigh. I rub the stubble dotting my chin. "What the hell is going on?"

"You're asking me?" Stu shoots out a string of four-letter words. "Why was your car found gutted in front of a strip joint?"

"I was trying to lose the press. Then I checked into a hotel to get some sleep." Even to my own ears the answer sounds stupid at best and pathetic at worst.

"And who's this hooker you were with last night?"

My features harden. "I wasn't with a hooker. You know that's not my style."

My agent's voice mocks me from the other end of the line. "You want to know what I do know about you, Ben? You're a fucking idiot. You just inherited twenty million bucks from a woman you had no business sleeping with—"

"Gretchen and I never—"

"So I told you to lay low, but did you listen? Oh no, you went out and caused a media storm. Do you realize how many calls I've gotten from the press this morning? Not to mention the police."

"Stu—"

"They think you were abducted by a crazed whore, for Christ's sake!"

"Stu—"

"Here's what we're going to do, Ben. I'll call Mary and have her fly to New York. She'll sit down with you and figure out a way to spin this so that you don't look like a complete jerk. But first we need to call off the cops and tell them Mr. Movie Star is alive and well. Capiche?"

"You're not Italian," I mutter.

"Capiche?" he repeats, sterner now.

"Whatever, sure. That sounds good. As for Mary, tell her to stay in LA. There's nothing to spin here."

"Are you insane?"

I grip the phone so tightly I fear it might shatter into a million little pieces. "I'm not insane. I'm just tired. I'm tired of being hounded and harassed and I haven't slept in a week, Stu. So go ahead and tell the police to call off their investigation, but don't expect me to make a solitary public appearance to explain this ridiculous story the press has yet again concocted."

"So, what, you're just going to fuel the fire by disappearing off the face of the earth?" Stu demands, sounding angrier than ever.

"That's exactly what I'm going to do. I'm going to disappear. You wanted me to lay low? Fine, I'll lay low. I'm not answering any calls, I'm not meeting with Mary or anyone from the PR firm. In fact, I'm not doing a fucking thing."

"What's that supposed to mean?"

"It means Ben Barrett is officially out of the limelight. For how long, I don't know. But I'm done, Stu. If I don't get some peace and quiet I'll end up in a nuthouse, so placate the cops, say whatever you want to the reporters and leave me the hell alone. *Capiche?*"

7

MAGGIE

"*B*ye, Maggie!"

I smile at the two little girls in the doorway before signing out at the community center where I volunteer. I wave at the counselor who doubles as a receptionist, give each of the giggling girls by the door a big hug good-bye and step outside.

Finally alone, I let out the weary sigh that's been lodged in my chest all afternoon.

Considering I got a grand total of three hours sleep last night, I probably should've skipped my shift and stayed in bed, but as usual, my irritating sense of responsibility prevented me from being lazy.

My work at the Joshua Broger Youth Center is more than just field placement for my degree. It's important to me, and I know the kids are disappointed when I don't show up—which is rare. Most of the children who come to the center live in foster homes, and having been a part of the foster system for thirteen years of my life, I only wish I'd had a place like the Broger Center to visit. Somewhere to get help with my homework, or talk to a counselor, or just spend some time with other children my age.

Volunteering, I feel like I'm making a difference. And I am. I know that.

But I wish I could make a difference and get paid for it at the same time.

The bottom line—I'm tired. Exhausted. So past exhausted I feel like an extra from a zombie movie.

It certainly doesn't help that instead of getting my quick Tony fix, I just ended up more frustrated than I'd been to begin with. And instead of banishing the embarrassing memories from my mind, I stayed up half the night thinking about my mysterious bad boy. If I were a braver woman, I might have stuck around and suggested we enjoy a few rounds of anonymous sex. At least then I wouldn't have spent the night lying in bed, aggravated and aching for release.

Sighing again, I approach the curb and focus on flagging down a taxi. I find one fairly quickly, though the drive back to Manhattan isn't as quick. I'm two minutes late when the driver maneuvers out of lane-to-lane Saturday evening traffic and finally creeps to a stop in front of the Olive. I hand the man a couple of bills, then hurry inside and make my way across the bar toward the employees' lounge.

"Hey, Trish," I call to the counter.

The second she sees me, Trisha drops the receipts in her hands and dashes over. "Walk faster," she hisses.

As she grabs my arm and practically drags me through the back corridor, I look at her with wide eyes. "What's the matter?"

"Just move."

Trisha pushes open the door to the lounge, staying on my heels as I head for the small bank of lockers at the far end of the room. I open my locker and shoot my co-worker a sideways glance.

"Well?"

She shifts from one foot to the other, her dark eyes dancing. "I think Ben Barrett is here."

I slip out of my jeans and change into the denim skirt the waitresses have to wear. "Who?"

"Who? Who? I can't believe you just asked me that. *Heart of a Hero*? *McLeod's Revenge*? *The Warrior*?"

I blink. "What, he writes romance novels or something?"

Trisha lets out a shriek. "No, you idiot. Those are movies he's starred in. You're honestly telling me you don't know who Ben Barrett is?"

I shrug, then pull my T-shirt over my head and exchange it for a V-neck black tank. "The name sounds familiar, but I can't attach a face to it." Kicking off my sneakers, I strap a pair of black heels on my feet and turn back to the enraged brunette.

"His latest action movie is in theaters right now!" she balks.

"Trish, the last time I went to the movies, I was ten. My foster parents took all the kids to see a Disney movie." I poke my tongue in my cheek. "Come to think of it, that's the only time I've gone to the movies."

"What about television?" she asks with a frustrated tilt of her chin. "You've got to watch TV."

"Not really." I pause. "If I'm not too tired, I'll watch sappy dramas with Summer. But lately we've been watching cooking shows. She's trying to learn about Jamaican cuisine so she can cook for Tygue. The first time she tried we all got food poisoning, so—"

"Forget it," Trisha cuts in, not looking amused. "All I'm going to say is I think a movie star is sitting in the booth near the pool table."

I don't really care, but I feel I owe it to my friend to ask, "What makes you think that?"

"Well, he came in about an hour ago, walked up to the bar

and ordered a glass of sparkling water. He gave Matt a hundred-dollar bill and said he wanted to be left alone."

"Gee, then it must be him."

Trisha ignores me. "He's wearing a baseball cap and hiding behind a newspaper, but he looks sooo familiar. I walked past him a few times and I swear it's him. And there's more."

"I can't wait to hear it."

"I saw on the news earlier that the police found Ben Barrett's car abandoned a few blocks from here."

"Maybe he couldn't find parking out front."

"Then," she continues, still ignoring me, "the cops gave a statement saying that Ben Barrett is alive and well, and he was just a victim of some good ol' NYC vandalism. But I think the whole thing was a scam, and he ditched his car because he's on the run."

My head begins to spin. "Why do you think I'm interested in any of this, Trish?"

"Because I need you to find out if it's him or not!" she wails.

"How would I know? I have no clue what the guy looks like, remember?"

"Well, I can't do it. I've already walked by his booth too many times. If I do it again it'll raise his suspicions and he'll take off."

I roll my eyes. I know Trisha is bored shitless with her boyfriend, and that sometimes her predicament causes her to poke her nose into other people's business. But this is just ridiculous.

As we leave the lounge, Trisha keeps pushing. "So will you find out if it's him?"

"Nope. Ask Matt."

"I did. He told me to leave the poor man alone."

"I second that notion." I stop at the counter and reach over it to retrieve an apron. Then I grin at the bartender. "Booth Five slipped you a hundred, huh?"

"Yep. And I suppose Trish told you she thinks he's a big star in disguise?" Matthew shoots her an annoyed look before growing serious. "Look, he said he doesn't want to be bothered, which is why I've been keeping this one"—Matt hooks a thumb at Trisha—"away from the poor guy."

Trisha glowers at him. "If you'd just let me go over there, I promise not to bug him."

"Yeah right," he hoots.

Lynda, our manager, walks up with a frown, and the good-natured bantering comes to a halt. Lynda isn't strict by any means, but her conservative nature and lack of humor turn off most of the staff.

No matter how grumpy she can be, I still like the older woman and greet her with a smile. "Hey, Lynda."

She ignores the greeting. "Guys, I've been here for an hour and not once has someone gone over to Booth Five to refill the customer's drink."

Looking sheepish, Matt opens his mouth to reply but Lynda silences him by holding up her hand. "You know I have no problem with the casual atmosphere we've created here, but we're going to need to change a few habits and start acting in a more professional manner. Jeremy is flying in next week to check on his investment, so it's time to shape up, all right?"

Jeremy Henderson is the owner of the Olive, but as far as I know, he's only stepped foot in this place half a dozen times since the grand opening. He leaves the day-to-day running of the bar to managers like Lynda, and the only sign that Henderson actually owns the Olive is his autograph on my paychecks.

I can see, though, why the owner's sudden decision to pop

in would unnerve Lynda, who's pretty much singled-handedly run the Olive for six years now.

"No problem," I assure my manager. I tie the pinstriped apron around my waist. "I'll check on Booth Five and see how he's doing."

As I head for the booth, I can feel Trisha's eyes boring into my back. I'd seen the flicker of irritation on my friend's face when I volunteered to handle it, but too bad. Considering Lynda just gave us a speech about professionalism, I don't think letting Trisha approach the alleged movie star is a good idea.

Like Trisha said, the mysterious stranger has his face hidden behind a newspaper, which really isn't all that suspicious when you think about it. People read newspapers every day. People read newspapers in bars every day. It doesn't mean they're celebrities.

"Sorry to disturb you, sir, but would you like some more water?" I ask the Sports section.

There's no response from the man behind the paper.

"Or maybe you'd like something else. A beer?"

Very slowly, the newspaper lowers.

A second later, my gaze collides with a pair of familiar blue eyes.

"Hello again," my stranger says pleasantly, the corner of his mouth lifting in a small grin.

"Oh," I squeak.

8

MAGGIE

*O*h? *Oh?* I can't think of anything better to say to the man I hopped into bed with last night?

I try to look casual despite the incessant thumping of my heart. God, I didn't think I'd see him again. Yet here he is.

And either I'm crazy, or I hadn't paid close enough attention yesterday, but he seems to have gotten even better looking. Has to be the clothes. Naked, he had sex written all over him. But now, in a leather jacket, white T-shirt, and faded blue jeans, he looks sexy and dangerous and completely edible.

As if the hotel-room disaster happened seconds ago rather than hours, my embarrassment returns with full force, slithers up my spine and settles in the back of my throat. Along with it, though, comes a spark of arousal at the memory of how incredible this guy's mouth felt on mine. How warm his hands were when they'd gripped my waist, and how hard his—

"No need to look so terrified," he quips, running a hand through his dark hair. "I won't bite, you know."

Yes, you will. You already did. I fight a shiver as I remember the way his teeth nibbled on my bottom lip.

"Um, I didn't think we'd see each other again." I lower my

37

voice so that nobody can overhear. "I guess you're here for that free drink."

"Actually, no." The other side of his mouth lifts so that a full-blown grin plays on his lips. "I'm here to return something."

"Return...?" I blush when I realize what he means. "Oh," I say, because once again it's the best I can come up with.

"I know how attached women can be to their panties." He winks. "Apparently it's like losing a limb."

Before I can answer, a sharp fingernail pokes the small of my back. The French-manicured perpetrator is Trisha, who gives a strangled cough that sounds like "ask him!" before she scurries away. Fucking hell.

But since I'd rather humor Trisha's farfetched suspicions than discuss my underwear, I lower my voice and ask, "Hey, so this is going to sound absolutely ridiculous, but is your name Ben Barrett?"

His grin fades. "Why do you ask?"

I shrug. "One of the waitresses here thinks you're Ben Barrett."

He doesn't answer.

"He's an actor," I add.

Still no answer. Wonderful. Have I just insulted him? Maybe he's one of those celebrity look-alikes who is constantly hassled on the streets and gets pissed off whenever somebody points out the resemblance.

Opening my mouth to apologize, I'm surprised when he meets my gaze and says, "Yes."

"Yes what?"

"I'm Ben Barrett."

The apology dies on my lips. Wait. What?

"The actor," he clarifies with a faint smile.

Clearly he's kidding.

Right?

Are you a reporter?

His question from last night floats into the forefront of my brain. Why had he asked that? Because, really, only a man who's used to having reporters around him would ask if I was one.

Which means...

Maybe he's not kidding?

I focus my wary gaze on his face. "Is this a joke?"

His features grow pained. "No."

"You're really this Ben Barrett guy?"

"Lower your voice, Red, will ya?"

Red?

"My name's Maggie," I say, absently playing with the hem of my apron. "And I don't get it. Why don't you want anyone to know who you are?"

"I..." He rubs his temples. "I don't want to be bothered. I've had a bitch of a time lately with reporters hounding me. I just want to be left alone."

I raise my eyebrows. "So you decided to come to one of the busiest bars in Manhattan on the busiest night of the week?"

He gives a shrug. "I wanted to see you."

My heart skips a beat. He wanted to see me?

"You don't even know me," I say slowly.

The grin returns to his rugged face. "Well, that can be easily changed." He says it in a voice so smooth with confidence and so heady with sexual promise, my body grows warm in response. No, not warm. Hot. Burning hot.

Hoping he can't see my nipples poking against my shirt, I swallow, desperate to allow some moisture back into my mouth. "I'm working."

I'm working? Again, that's all I can come up with? What about, *Look, you're hot but I don't have time for complications right now.*

Because I'm pretty sure Ben Barrett would be just that—a

complication. He might be sexy as sin, and yeah, his voice gives me shivers that are completely foreign to me, but there's no doubt in my mind that this man is trouble.

I don't have time to play games with a movie star, no matter how delicious he looks. That's why I prefer guys like Tony. Tony doesn't have time for games. Or much of anything, for that matter. With him, it's simply, let's have some hot sex and see you later.

"I'm fully aware that you're working," Ben says. "But I've waited tables myself before, so I'm pretty sure you'll have a break in a couple hours, right?"

I nod. "Nine o'clock."

He returns the nod. "Good. So we'll talk then."

"We will, huh?" I arch one eyebrow.

"Yep."

I narrow my eyes. How arrogant is this guy? He just assumes I'll spend my dinner break hanging out with him? Like I have no other options? Like his sex appeal is so strong I just can't wait to be alone with him and—

"I'll meet you out front at nine," I grumble.

Then I head back to the counter and try to convince myself that his good looks and sexy voice have absolutely no effect on me.

9

BEN

I smother a laugh as I watch Maggie scurry away. I wonder if she realizes her tendency to blush pretty much eliminates any chance of covering up her emotions. I've only been around her twice, but I'm able to pick up on everything she's feeling from that telltale blush on her cheeks.

Crimson red means she's embarrassed. I saw it last night, and again today, when I brought up the subject of her panties.

Scarlet means she's angry, which was evident when I announced we'd be meeting up during her break.

And rosy pink...well, that's a clear and undeniable shade of arousal.

She's attracted to me. I know it, and I'm pretty sure she knows it too. Hell, it would be damn hard to deny it, seeing as the sexual tension hissed like a rattlesnake the second our eyes met.

I take a sip of water and reach for the novel I tucked into the pocket of my jacket. Nine o'clock, she'd said. Leaves me with a few hours to kill, but that's why I bought the book. I tried reading it earlier in Central Park, but I was too tense and too alert. Losing myself in a thriller was hard when I was constantly glancing over my shoulder, waiting for someone to ask for an autograph, or for a photographer to pop out from the other side of the bike path and snap my picture.

Maybe that's why I came here tonight. I know sooner or later I'll have to figure out where to spend the night, but calling up the few acquaintances I know in the city or attempting to check into another hotel appeals to me as much as having my chest waxed.

Why should I risk it anyway? My so-called friends would sell me out in a nanosecond. And if the other hotel clerks in Manhattan are anything like the guy from the Lester, I would only find myself on the news again.

I thought about renting a car and driving upstate, maybe checking into a little B & B, but something stopped me from leaving the city.

No, not something. Someone.

More specifically, the curvy redhead whose green eyes keep darting in my direction.

Fuck, she looks even sexier now that I'm fully awake. All that silky red hair that can't decide if it wants to be wavy or straight. Her emerald eyes. Tight body. Looking at her now, I wish I asked her to stay last night. Would've been a lot more fun than the self-gratification session I had to indulge in after she left me with a raging hard-on.

Although I can't really explain it, this woman has been on my mind from the second I opened his eyes this morning, and now I'm glad I listened to the strange urge that told me to come see her. I've been on edge all day, but sitting here in this booth with nothing to do but read a book and wait for Maggie to go on break, I don't feel as stiff. The tension in my back has eased, my muscles are relaxed, and for the first time in a long time I'm relishing the feeling of being anonymous.

From the corner of my eye, I see Maggie exchange a few

words with the brown-haired waitress who's been eyeing me all evening. The sight of the two women whispering causes a sliver of unease to pierce through me. Are they talking about me?

More importantly, is Maggie confirming my identity or denying it?

The latter becomes likelier, as Maggie's fellow waitress frowns, then pouts, then glances over at me with supreme disappointment.

I stick my nose in my book to hide a smile. Maggie covered for me. Why, though? She really had no reason to do that, but the fact that she respected my request for privacy pleases me.

When she sidles past my booth again, I can't help but shoot her a grateful smile. She doesn't smile back, just spares a brief look in my direction and saunters by.

Is that annoyance in her gaze?

I twist around and watch as she maneuvers through the large, dimly lit bar, which is beginning to fill up. Most of the scattered tables and wall-to-wall booths are occupied, and a popular hip-hop song now blares from the speaker system. Since it's Saturday night, I know the place will soon be filled to capacity, but I can't bring myself to duck out just yet.

I'm far too fascinated with the redhead across the room.

Her ass looks delicious in her short denim skirt, making my hand tingle with the urge to squeeze it. My gaze drifts north, to her slim back and the wavy red hair cascading down it. I'm startled to find my dick hardening at the sight.

Jeez. When was the last time I got an erection from the sight of a woman's back?

Lowering my eyes to the novel, I try to shake off the desire raging in my blood, but my senses kick into overdrive as I remember every detail from last night. How sweet her hair smelled when it brushed against my cheek. The heat of her body pressed against mine. The taste of her lips. The urgency of her tongue. The way her pussy tightened over my finger when I slid it inside her.

The mouth-watering memories only make it more difficult to keep my cock in check. Eventually, I close the book and glance at my watch. Quarter to nine. Man, time sure flies when you're fantasizing about a hot redhead while pretending to read.

"Do you think it's him?" hisses a high-pitched female voice.

Shit.

Even in my fairly isolated booth, I know the two women by the counter have a clear view of me. I tug on my baseball cap at the same time I hear four words that make me cringe.

"It's totally Ben Barrett."

My muscles stiffen again, as my brain orders me to get out before the girls at the bar decide to approach me.

Maggie's throaty voice stops me from rising.

"Sorry, honey, it's not who you think it is." She gives a loud, exaggerated sigh that makes my lips twitch. "I thought it was him too, but it's not. I already asked."

"That sucks," says one of the women. "I heard he's in the city."

"If he is, he wouldn't come to a place like this." From my vantage point, I notice the smile on Maggie's lips seems forced. "Big celebrities like him get suites at the Plaza and do blow with high-class call girls."

I choke back a laugh. I'm tempted to march over there and kiss her senseless as thanks for covering for me. Or maybe not as thanks. Maybe I just want to kiss her.

Instead, I wait patiently for another fifteen minutes, then stand up when I hear Maggie tell the bartender she'll be back in thirty.

Tucking my book in my pocket, I hop out of the booth and head for the door.

I breathe in the late evening air. A few moments later,

Maggie walks out of the bar. She pauses near the streetlight by the curb, the pale yellow light causing her hair to appear redder and brighter. Like a halo of fire kindled by the evening breeze.

"Hey." I greet her with a faint smile.

She stares me down with obvious wariness. And there it is again, a gleam of annoyance. What the hell is up with that?

"Hi." She holds on to the thick strap of her oversized purse. "I have a half hour for my dinner break. I usually grab a hot dog."

"Let's go," I say easily.

She nods and then pushes forward, her high heels clacking against the pavement.

I fall into step with her and cock my head. "You look angry."

She shoots me a sideways glance. "What makes you think that?"

I shrug. "Are you?"

"A little."

"Because I showed up at your work?"

Her hands drop to her hips as she stops walking. "Yes. Thanks to you, I've spent the past three hours as your bodyguard, trying to keep every vagina in the place away from you."

I have to grin. "I never asked you to do that."

"You didn't have to. You turned white as mayo when I asked who you were. It was obvious you didn't want to be bothered." She pauses. "Besides, I owe you. Celebrity or not, I still barged into your room last night."

With a frown, she resumes walking. I quicken my pace to keep up with her, oddly pleased that my celebrity status is an obvious thorn in her side.

It sure as hell is a thorn in mine.

"So what do you want?"

She gets right to the point, which I suspect she does a lot.

Just another item to add to my already growing list of reasons why I like her.

"I told you, I came to return something."

We stop in front of a hot dog vendor, who Maggie greets by name. She orders a dog with all the fixings, pays the man, and turns back to me.

"So that's it? You came by to return my underwear?"

A loud cough sounds. I glance over to find the hot dog vendor raising his bushy eyebrows at us.

Maggie waves a dismissive hand. "Just a figure of speech, Joe. Pretend you didn't hear that."

She says good-bye and gestures for me to follow her. Moments later we're leaning against a brick wall a few yards away, and I can't help but be impressed as I watch Maggie eat.

It's been a while since I've met a woman who dined in anything less than a five-star restaurant. If I even dared to suggest to a date we indulge in some street meat I'd probably get slapped. But Maggie looks completely comfortable as she scarfs down a hot dog and wipes ketchup from the corner of her delectable mouth.

She doesn't seem to notice the people hurrying by or the sound of cars whizzing down Broadway. When a cop car speeds past, sirens blazing, she doesn't even blink. She acts like having dinner in the middle of a busy street is no big deal.

"Is there a reason why you're staring at me like that?" she asks politely.

"I like the way you eat."

One reddish-brown eyebrow lifts. "Is that some weird pick-up line?"

A laugh slips out. "No, just an honest-to-God compliment. It's been a while since I hung out with a woman who ate something other than a side salad."

Maggie makes a face as she swallows the last bite of her hot dog. "If my meals consisted of side salads, I'd die of malnutrition." She wipes her mouth with a napkin and then tosses it in a nearby trashcan. "Anyway. Listen up, Mr. Movie Star."

I can't help but grin. "I'm all ears."

"What do you want from me? I already apologized for last night and you passed on my offer for a free drink, so why are you here?" Before I can answer, she narrows those emerald eyes. "You're not going to sue me, are you?"

I'm taken aback. "What?"

"Sue me. For sexual harassment or something."

"Of course I'm not going to sue you."

"You better not." She scowls at me. "It would never hold up in court, anyway."

I stare at her, bewildered. Who is this woman? One minute she's angry with me, the next she's accusing me of launching a potential lawsuit. It's exasperating, but in a cute way, and as I stand there gaping at her, I finally figure out what's drawing me to her.

It isn't the fact that she's oblivious to my career, or the way her curvy body felt pressed against mine. It isn't the appealing blushing, or the killer legs, or how great her ass looks in that short skirt.

I like her because she treats me like a...human being.

She knows who I am now, and she still doesn't care. She isn't trying to impress me, isn't holding her tongue. Aside from my mother, this redheaded waitress is the first woman who isn't scared to tell me exactly what she's thinking.

"Okay, so what do you want?" she repeats, her lips pursed in irritation. "And don't say a date, because I really don't have time for that."

I laugh again and decide this is the best conversation I've ever had with a girl.

"What do I want," I say thoughtfully. I pull one hand out of my pocket and with it comes her pink panties. With a chivalrous bow, I hand her the silky underwear. "First, to return these. I don't want your pretty little butt getting cold."

A whisper of a smile crosses her mouth as she tucks the underwear into her purse. "My butt is just fine, Mr. Barrett. I do own more than one pair of panties. And second?"

"Second?"

"You said the underwear was first. What's second?"

I poke my tongue in my cheek and eye her, experiencing one of those rare moments when words escape me. What do I want? Well, I know what I need, and that's to figure out where to spend the night without ending up on the news again.

What I want, though, is to pull this chick into my arms and kiss the hell out of her. And then maybe go back to her place and fuck the hell out of her.

Then again...who says that my needs and wants are mutually exclusive?

I need a bed.

I want this woman in bed with me.

Why can't I have both?

"You're doing it again," Maggie accuses, jolting me back to reality.

"Doing what?"

"Staring at me. Be honest, do I have something stuck between my teeth?"

I laugh. "No."

"Then quit staring. It's rude." She shakes her head in exasperation. "Okay, we've wasted enough time here. I have to go back to work and you—"

I cut her off. "Let me stay at your place tonight."

10

MAGGIE

*M*y jaw closes so abruptly I can hear a few teeth rattling around in my mouth. Is this man insane? *Let me stay at your place tonight.*

Seven words I never expected to hear, and yet the second he says them a thrill shoots up my spine.

Fine, so maybe the idea of bringing this sex god home is seriously tempting. But unlike most people, I'm pretty skilled at resisting temptation.

I stare into Ben's dark blue eyes and wonder if he's joking. He doesn't look like it. No amusement on his face, just a dead-serious expression.

Does he actually think I'm going to let him stay at my apartment?

"No offense or anything, but are you strapped for cash?" I ask carefully. The guy's financial situation isn't any of my business, but I have to know.

"No, I'm doing all right in the finance department."

He takes a step back, but I still feel the heat radiating from his lean body. His leather jacket doesn't emphasize his muscled arms or rippled chest, but I remember those details well. I wonder if he has any other tattoos I might have missed in the dark. Then I wonder why my thighs are trembling at the idea there might be more.

For God's sake, stop checking him out and focus.

Right. It doesn't matter how many tattoos might be hidden on that hard body of his. That's no reason to invite him to stay with me.

"Okay, so you've got money," I say, crossing my arms over my chest. "Which means you can afford to check into a hotel."

"I'd much rather stay with you, Red."

"Are you in trouble with the law?"

"No. I just need a place to sleep. It'll only be for a few days."

My jaw drops. "A few *days*?"

"Yeah." He gives me a little boy look. "Is that a yes?"

"No!" I'm still gawking at him. "Why not a hotel?"

"Do you always ask so many questions?" he counters.

"When a stranger asks to crash at my place, yes."

"We're not strangers." He moves closer and dips his head so we're at eye level. "We've been in bed together, remember?"

He has to bring that up again, doesn't he?

"I just don't get why you're asking me this."

He sighs, and his warm breath tickles the bridge of my nose. "Here's the short version—I haven't slept in days because the press is on my back for a silly scandal they fabricated. This morning they thought I was abducted. The cops gave a statement that I wasn't, but the media is still camped out in front of my building."

"No friends you could call?"

"Friends?" He makes a bitter noise that sounds like a cross between a laugh and a snort. "Let me enlighten you about my so-called friends. A guy I grew up with—we were inseparable since we were six years old, I was best man at his wedding. Last year he sold pictures of me from his bachelor party for a quarter million. Sound like a friend to you?"

I swallow. "Ouch." Then, realizing I've let my sympathy distract me, I mutter, "All right, so you've succeeded in making me feel sorry for you."

"I don't expect you to feel sorry—"

"But it doesn't mean you can coax a free bed out of me."

He lowers his head again so that his lips brush my ear. "I doubt you need much coaxing. It's obvious you want me in your bed as much as I want to be there."

"Excuse me?" A spark of anger lights my stomach at the sheer arrogance dripping from his tone. "Where do you get off?"

A lazy grin spreads across his mouth. "Well, last night, I got off while fantasizing about a certain redhead."

Heat rolls through me.

"Tonight, though," he says with that wicked grin, "I figured maybe we'd get off together."

My arousal is joined by another flicker of anger. Guys are never this forward with me, and although his flirting is kind of amusing, the way he assumes he can just snap his fingers and get me into bed is insulting.

"Look, I get it. You apparently think you're God's gift to women. But let me tell you something, Ben Barrett—I'm not one of those girls who swoons in the presence of a celebrity, okay? In fact, the last thing I want to do is get involved with someone like—"

He kisses me.

Just like that. No permission, no warning, he just slams his hot mouth on mine and kisses me.

If any other man did this, I would probably slug him, but I find myself unable to pull away. Like last night, he doesn't take the time to be gentle. He parts my lips with his tongue, while his hands drift down to my waist to keep me against him. And just when I begin to respond, just when my tongue flicks against his and the fingers of my right hand slide into his dark hair, he pulls back.

And grins at me.

"Know what that was?" he says cheerfully.

I struggle to catch my breath. "A totally insensitive way to shut me up?"

"Our first fight." He drops his hands from my hips and sticks them back in his pockets. "So, when are you off work, Red?"

All I can do is stare at him. Are all movie stars this crazy or is it just this particular one?

"I'm done at two," I find myself replying. "Why?"

He ignores the question. "I'll meet you here when you're done. You can give me your answer then."

"My answer?"

"About letting me crash with you."

"I already said—"

He presses his index finger to my lips, which causes a shiver to dance up my spine. "Think about it. That's all I ask. Give me your answer after you've had a chance to do that." He shoots me that cocky smile again. "Not that there's much to think about. You and I both know exactly where I'll be spending the night, don't we, Maggie?"

11

BEN

*W*omen don't say no to me.

It's simply one of the delicious facts of life that I've come to accept over the years. Even before I started acting, the ladies loved me. Hell, when I was fifteen, a few friends dared me to ask the most popular senior in school to the freshman prom, and not only had I walked into the high school gym with the hottest girl on my arm, but I also lost my virginity that night.

Needless to say, I'm not surprised when Maggie walks out of the bar at two a.m. and gestures for me to follow her.

Yup, I still have a way with the ladies.

And yet while Maggie clearly isn't saying no, she's the first chick I've encountered who has the nerve to look less than pleased with her decision to say yes.

"I'm not going to stay at your place if you sulk all night," I say, keeping my stride casual as I follow her down the sidewalk.

It's late, and the Saturday night crowds have finally started to disperse. In the distance, a thin mist shrouds the buildings and skyscrapers, and the spring air is chilled, causing me to zip up my jacket. When I glance over at Maggie, my gaze doesn't miss the way her nipples are poking against the thin bra under the blue long-sleeved shirt she now wears. She's also changed into a pair of snug blue jeans and tied her long hair into a low ponytail, which makes her seem younger.

"I'm not sulking," she replies, her frown deepening.

"Sure you are." I stick my hands in my pockets and cock my head at her. "I actually find it quite insulting."

She stops walking. "You want to know what's insulting? You assuming you can waltz into my life and expect me to agree to whatever tickles your fancy."

I lift a brow. "Considering we're on the way to your apartment, I'd say that wasn't a bad assumption."

Her cheeks turn bright red. "The only reason I'm letting you stay over is because I feel sorry for you," she huffs.

A laugh trickles out of my mouth. "Sure, babe. If you say so."

We fall into step again, me still chuckling, and Maggie apparently using silence as punishment for my amusement. I wonder how she'd react if I tell her I view her silence as a reward. If I tell her she's the first woman who doesn't fawn all over me or coddle me. The women who tend to pursue me are vacuous fame chasers, trying to seduce me to further their own ambitions.

Not that I don't like being seduced. Every now and then, however, I like the challenge of doing the seducing myself. A rare luxury, considering most women are ready to fuck me before I even ask. Hell, these days I don't even have to ask.

"This is it," Maggie says, breaking the drawn-out silence as we come to a stop in front of an older-looking high-rise with large balconies.

She uses a key to get into the lobby, then heads for the

elevator without looking back to see if I'm following. It's kinda cute, the way she pretends she's doing me a favor by letting me come home with her. I know better, of course. The way she trembled against me during the kiss earlier proves the attraction between us is very mutual.

"How long have you lived here?" I ask as we step into the elevator.

She shoots me a dirty look. "Don't make small talk."

"Why not?"

"Because you're only wasting time." The doors open with a loud buzz, and Maggie whisks out of the car, over her shoulder adding, "Neither of us has any illusions about why you're here."

The remark startles me, so much so that the elevator nearly closes on my toes. I push forward before the doors shut and hurry after Maggie. Another first, having to chase after a woman.

"And what's that supposed to mean?" I catch up to her as she unlocks the door to her apartment.

"It means we both know how this night is going to end," she replies, mocking me with my earlier words.

Any other time I would have a sexy comeback, but the second I enter Maggie's apartment, I become speechless.

"This is where you live?" I finally demand. I'm gaping at her.

"Yeah. Is there a problem?"

There isn't a problem, but I certainly hadn't expected *this*. If I hadn't seen Maggie unlock the door, I would think we were in the wrong apartment.

The place looks like somebody's grandmother lives in it. The furniture, mostly plaid upholstery, is all mismatched. The paintings on the wall depict bland landscapes and the occasional kitten rolling around in a garden. Frilly pink tablecloths and doilies that appear handmade cover every table in the room, and I have to blink a few times to be sure, but I think I see photos of Cary Grant and a young Marlon Brando hanging over the TV.

The only item in the apartment that resembles anything modern is the steel drum sitting in the open-concept dining room, but I can't quite figure that out either.

When I finish my scrutiny, I glance over and see the humor dancing in Maggie's eyes.

"C'mon, say it," she taunts.

"What?"

"How tacky it is. We both know you want to say it."

I might've been living in Hollywood for the past ten years of my life, but I grew up in Ohio with a mother who'd instilled good manners in me. "It's not tacky," I lie. "Did you decorate it yourself?"

Laughter bubbles out of her throat. "Wow. Did you learn the art of bullshitting from the film industry or does it just come naturally to you?"

"What? No, I think this place is really something." Something terrifying.

She laughs again. "Relax, Barrett. I didn't decorate it. My roommate's grandmother owns this place. When she moved, she made Summer promise not to change a thing."

My ears perk. "You have a roommate?"

Her amused expression quickly dissolves into another frown. "Summer's gone for the week—and she has a boyfriend. So wipe any sleazy notions of a threesome out of your head."

How is it humanly possible that she keeps catching me off-guard like this?

My nostrils flare as I ponder the best way to respond. "You really don't think much of me, do you?"

"I don't even know you."

"You're right, you don't." I offer a shrug. "For what it's worth, the reason I asked about your roommate is because I wanted to make sure we'd be alone."

"Well, we are." Sighing, she crosses her arms. "So let's just do this, okay?"

"Do what?"

"Let's have sex."

"No thanks." I unzip my jacket and shrug it off my shoulders. "So, should I sleep on the couch or is there a spare room?"

"Excuse me?" She drops her arms and lets them dangle at her sides. "Did you just say 'no thanks'?"

I toss my jacket on a nearby armchair. "That's right, I did."

When I meet her gaze, she has the gall to look confused. "You don't want to have sex?"

"Not when you act like it's a chore."

Another sigh tumbles out of her mouth, longer this time, and lined with exasperation. "I can't believe you. You've been flirting with me all night, taunting me about how it's inevitable we're going to end up in bed together, and when I finally give in, you back out?"

Shaking her head, she stalks past me toward the kitchen. A large window has been cut out of the wall, so I can see her every movement as she pulls the fridge door open so hard that the items on the shelves clatter against one another. I hide a grin, enjoying her visible indignation.

She's pissed and I love it. Not that I get off on infuriating women, but this one deserves to have a few feathers ruffled. I'm used to people making assumptions about me, but Maggie is the first woman to openly challenge and criticize me. Also, the first woman who acts like having sex with me is equivalent to having a root canal—which ain't cool. Or great for my ego.

"Why did you ask me to come here when it's obviously not

what you want?" I roll my eyes as I approach the kitchen doorway.

She pours a glass of orange juice and then sips the liquid slowly. I notice that the fire has left her eyes, replaced by a flicker of hesitation.

"It is what I want," she finally replies.

Her expression is so glum that my ego takes another nice hit. "Don't sound so enthusiastic."

"You don't get it." She plays with the edge of her ponytail, and the vulnerability moving across her face chips away at my irritation. "I don't have much room in my life for dating." She gives a self-deprecating smile. "Or sex."

"And yet our first meeting took place in a hotel room, with you getting naked and hopping into my bed." I take a step closer, but still keep a few feet between us. "Who were you supposed to meet?"

"Tony." Her reply comes out as a groan.

The spark of jealousy I feel at the sound of another man's name on Maggie's lips is not only unwelcome, but bewildering. "And who's Tony?"

She stares down at her high heels. "Just a guy I meet a couple times a year."

"Not a boyfriend?"

"No. Like I said, I don't have time for dating. Or sex," she repeats.

As understanding dawns, I give an amazed laugh. "Are you saying you only have sex two times a year, with this Tony guy?"

"Sometimes it's three," she says, sounding defensive.

Another laugh tickles my throat. I try very hard to swallow it back. For the first time all night, Maggie has dropped her combative attitude. The last thing I want is to spark another fight by making fun of her.

"What exactly keeps you so busy?" I ask, genuinely curious.

"Work. School. Volunteering." She shrugs. "Relationships always seem to get in the way. That's why I don't understand this."

"This?" I echo.

"You. This attraction I have to you." She rubs her forehead, then her temples, then pinches the bridge of her nose, as if acknowledging the chemistry between us is nothing but a headache. "I don't bring guys home. I don't have flings. I don't have *time* for flings. Especially with men like you."

Against my better sense, a grin lifts the corners of my mouth. "And what kind of man am I?"

She glowers at me. "The complicated kind. The distracting kind."

"Interesting. What is it about me that distracts you?" I close the distance between us and plant my hands on her waist. "Let me guess. I distract you because—much as it bugs you—I turn you on like nobody's business. Am I right?

"No."

I chuckle. "It's okay to be in denial. And it's also okay to feel disappointed."

She pushes my hands off her. "Why would I feel disappointed?"

"Because the ship has sailed."

"What ship?"

"The sex ship." I cross my arms. "You blew it, Red."

"Excuse me?" Both her eyebrows sail up to her forehead, and I feel like kissing that indignant frown off her sexy mouth.

But I don't.

"You heard me. You missed your chance." I poke the inside of my cheek with my tongue and fight back a grin. "I'm sorry to inform you—I won't be fucking you tonight."

"*Wow*. You are the most egotistical—"

"Enough small talk," I cut in with a pleasant smile. "Will you be showing me to my room or should I just take the couch?"

12

MAGGIE

*I*s it possible to hate a man and want to rip off his clothes at the same time?

I've been pondering the question all morning, but the answer still eludes me. What remains clear, however, is that on the one-to-ten scale of sexual frustration, I'm sitting at eleven right about now.

As the sunlight streams in through the open window blinds, I slide up into a sitting position and lean against the headboard, wondering if Ben slept as horribly as I did. Probably not. Knowing him, he dreamt of kittens and rainbows all night long, unfazed by everything that happened.

I, on the other hand, spent eight hours tossing and turning and fighting the urge to jump out of bed and jump Ben Barrett's bones.

God, I acted like a spoiled brat last night.

Try bitch.

Fine, I'll call a spade a spade.

When I brought Ben back to the apartment, I truly had every intention of having some fun with him. But then we walked inside, and the first thing I saw was the pile of textbooks on the computer desk. The stack of bills on the hall table. The jam-packed schedule tacked on the fridge.

Then I looked over and there was Ben. A gorgeous, confident man who made it clear he wanted to tear off my clothes with his teeth. A man who kissed like a champion and made me feel dizzy with desire.

That's when the confusion kicked in. Somehow this cocky movie star managed to make important tasks like studying and paying bills seem secondary. And then, to make matters worse, when I let down my guard and admitted I don't usually make time for sex, Ben had backed off. Just when I'd been ready to stop acting like an uptight party-pooper—*fine, bitch*—he'd promptly taken sex off the table and gone to bed. Alone.

I guess I deserve that.

Yawning, I glance at the clock on my bedside table. Ten thirty. I can't remember the last time I got up later than eight, and the realization that I've wasted half my morning stewing over Ben's rejection and my own stupidity isn't one I like waking up with.

The faint sound of music finally draws me out of my warm covers. I wrinkle my forehead as I search for my slippers, the fuzzy, pink cat ones the kids at the center collectively bought me last year for my birthday. I find them in front of the closet, slip my bare feet into them, and leave the bedroom.

In the narrow hall, the music grows louder. Sounds like...the Beach Boys? Yep, it's the Beach Boys, I realize as the soft strains of "I Get Around" become clear. Then I make out a male voice humming along and roll my eyes. Hard. Of course Ben is listening to this. It's probably his life's theme song.

I find him in the kitchen, frying eggs over the stove and singing along with the song playing on his cell phone, which he set up on the work island in the middle of the room.

I open my mouth to utter a crack about making himself at home, but the words die in my throat the second he turns around.

He's barefoot and bare-chested, wearing nothing but a pair of jeans that ride low on his lean hips. His dark hair sports a serious case of bedhead, and the stubble on his chin is thicker, giving him a masculine sexiness that causes heat to simmer in my belly.

My gaze drifts to his tattoos, the tribal designs and lines and lines of text that I can't read from where I'm standing. My pulse quickens when I glance south again and note the absence of a second waistband. Is he not wearing any boxers?

Ugh. Why does this man have to be so damn...fuckable?

"Finished gawking?"

His rough voice causes my head to snap up. Ben's grinning at me, looking totally pleased by the fact that I've been checking him out.

"I wasn't gawking," I lie, breezing toward the fridge to get some orange juice. "I was just—"

"Shhh." He holds up his hand to silence me, cocks his head toward the phone, and starts singing the first few lines of "Barbara Ann."

Open-mouthed, I just stare at him, waiting until he tires of the song and turns his attention back to the sunny-side eggs sizzling in the pan.

"I take it you're a Beach Boys fan," I say, sipping my juice. I set down the glass so I can run my fingers through my frizzy, slept-on hair.

It's slightly unnerving having him here, cooking breakfast in nothing but a pair of jeans. Tony and I never do the breakfast thing, or the morning thing, or any thing that doesn't involve hot sex followed by goodbye.

"The biggest," he replies, shooting me a toe-curling grin before reaching over to turn off the stove.

Using a spatula, he drops one egg on a plate, followed by a piece of brown toast, and hands it to me. "Enjoy."

When was the last time a man cooked for me?

Oh right. Never.

Oddly touched, I take the plate, and settle on the lone stool by the counter. The kitchen is too small to be considered "eat-in" on any real estate listing, and I'm about to suggest moving to the dining room when Ben picks up his own plate, leans against the counter, and starts eating standing up. Well. At least he isn't one of those celebrities who expects to be served while he sits on a throne.

"You know, I dated a girl named Barbara Ann once," he says after he's swallowed a bite of toast.

"Doesn't surprise me." I chew slowly. "I bet you've also dated a Rhonda, and every other girl the Beach Boys sing about. You've also dated every actress and model in the eighteen to thirty-five demographic."

"What makes you say that?"

"I Googled you last night."

"No, you didn't. We slept in separate bedrooms."

I roll her eyes. "I couldn't sleep, so I researched you."

Winking, he polishes off the rest of his breakfast. To my surprise, he washes his dish and sets it to dry on the plastic tray on the counter, then leaves the frying pan in the sink to soak. Wow. Even Summer doesn't do her dishes this quickly, and I've dubbed her the ultimate neat-freak.

"Why couldn't you sleep?" Ben asks.

"I just told you I researched you and you want to know why I couldn't sleep?"

"Yep." He grins. "So why couldn't you?"

I was too busy fantasizing about licking every inch of your body. "I was too tired."

"Right." It's obvious he doesn't believe me.

"Anyway," I go on, hoping he'll leave it at that, "it turns out you're quite the playboy."

I don't mention the unwelcome pang of jealousy I experienced while reading about Ben Barrett's conquests. Considering the only type of appearance Ben will be making in my world is a cameo, I have no idea what to make of the claws that came out when I saw all those photos of him with other women.

He looks insulted. "I'm not a playboy."

"Sure you are. You travel the world and have casual affairs with gorgeous women. That makes you a playboy." I quirk an eyebrow. "Or would you prefer fuckboy?"

He raises an eyebrow right back. "Well, with you getting laid only twice a year, I can see why my reputation might intimidate you."

"Sometimes three times," I correct. Then I scowl. "You really are one of those annoyingly cheerful morning people, aren't you?"

"I sure am."

He waits while I shove the last mouthful of eggs into my mouth, and then takes my plate. To my surprise, he washes it as well.

"Don't tell me you dated Martha Stewart too," I grumble.

Ben wipes his hands with a pink dishcloth. "No, but I grew up with one. My mother never let me leave the kitchen until it was spotless." As if to punctuate that, he uses the dishcloth to wipe the counter until it squeaks. "So what are we doing today?"

The question catches me off-guard, but I quickly cover up

my surprise. "Well, I have a ton of stuff to do, and you, I assume, will be finding a hotel. Or maybe you'll be talking with your publicity people about your recent scandal. I read about that too, by the way."

His cheerful expression fades. "You did?"

"Yep. So that rich lady left you her money, huh?"

I hit a nerve. I can tell from the way his features harden and his eyes narrow into slits. I'd only managed to dig up a few details about Ben's involvement with Gretchen Goodrich, but enough to suspect how touchy a subject it must be.

Goodrich was the heiress to a salad dressing empire and wife of an Academy Award-winning director. She lost the battle with breast cancer three months ago, and from what I read she'd left Ben close to twenty million dollars in her will. The press hinted at an affair between Ben and the fifty-three-year-old, but since there doesn't seem to be any actual evidence of it, I've decided it's most likely a rumor. Still, Ben must have been pretty close to the woman if she'd left him a part of her fortune.

"You can't believe everything you read," Ben says in a mild tone. The frown leaves his face, but his stiff posture tells me he's still on edge.

Before I can say anything else, he breezes past me, bare feet padding against the tiled floor. I figure he's heading to Summer's room to get dressed, so when he flops down on the couch and reaches for the remote control, I bolt to my feet and scurry into the living room.

"What are you doing?" I demand. "I just told you, I've got tons of stuff to do."

"I'll wait." He flips on the TV and turns it to ESPN.

"You can't." Exasperation climbs up my chest. "I have a really busy day."

Ben presses the mute button and shoots me an expectant look. "Doing what?"

"You want me to write you a list?"

"No, a verbal break-down would be fine."

Oh, I'll give him a verbal break-down, all right. I don't care how sexy he looks in those jeans or how enticing his chest is. It's Sunday, and Sunday is *my* day. The only day I don't work or volunteer or take notes in a classroom. Sure, I spend the free time cleaning and doing homework, but it's free time nonetheless.

"I need to finish writing a paper," I say, setting my jaw. "Then I have to research child abuse law and make notes so I can write another paper. Then I need to study for exams." I take a breath. "And after I've done all that, I was going to wax my legs. Satisfied?"

He furrows his brow. "Why do you wax your legs when the only guy who sees them comes to town twice a year?"

"Sometimes three times," I snap. "And I don't need to justify my leg-waxing routines to you. So get dressed and go do some movie star things, like, I don't know, golfing or staring at your reflection in store windows."

His answering laughter sounds like honeyed sandpaper. "Is that what you think movie stars do?"

"I don't care what you do," I growl, starting to grow annoyed. "I just want you to go away. My schoolwork requires silence."

"So I'll be quiet." He shrugs and directs his attention back to the sports highlight reel on TV.

It takes all my willpower not to pull my own hair out by the roots. What does he want from me? Obviously not sex, considering he hasn't touched me since last night.

"You're seriously not going to leave?" My voice is a cross between a squeak and a groan, with another growl thrown in for good measure.

His blue eyes never leave the screen. "Nope."

"But...I...you..." I groan irritably. "Just keep the volume down!"

Spinning on my heel, I storm into my bedroom and curse myself for not being strong enough to physically throw him out. As I get dressed, I hear him chuckling from the other room.

13

BEN

*B*ecause I've taken a vow of silence, I spend most of the afternoon fighting back laughter and watching TV with the volume off and the captions on. In the dining room, Maggie sits at the table, typing away on her laptop and stopping every now and then to rustle through the pages of a textbook the size of an encyclopedia.

She's been working for hours, her eyes glued to the monitor, her fingers on the keyboard. And the way she keeps biting her bottom lip in concentration makes me want to walk over there and capture that pouty lip with my teeth.

I'm not really sure why I'm forcing my presence on her, especially after last night. If any other woman had grumbled that much about the idea of fucking me, I would've just said goodbye and moved on. So why am I still here?

I don't know if pursuing a woman who views sex as a complication is even worth the hassle. I mean, I have nothing against playing hard to get, but in Maggie's case, it goes beyond a coy little game. Under normal circumstances, I'd pass on the challenge and focus my energy on a woman who actually wants to be around me, but there's nothing normal about this situation. Or about Maggie.

Since I've met her, I've barely thought about the scandal hanging over my head, or the fact that reporters are camped outside my home. Thanks to this infuriating woman, I've managed to think about something other than my own troubles, and I kind of want to hang on to that liberating feeling for a while longer.

"You should take a break." I speak before I can help it, hoping Maggie won't reprimand me for breaking my oath of silence.

"I just have to write my conclusion," she says without turning around. She taps a few keys with her fingers. "Give me a sec."

I try to tell myself I'm not thinking of my own needs as I rise from the couch and walk toward her. Instead, I focus on the fact that Maggie has been working for five hours straight without so much as a bathroom break.

Standing behind her, I place my hands on her shoulders and start rubbing the knot between her shoulder blades. She flinches for a second and then leans into my massaging fingers, sighing softly.

"See, you need a break," I chide. "You're so stiff."

And boy, do I know what stiff feels like. Although the material of her long-sleeved shirt is woven from thick cotton, I can feel the heat of her skin underneath my fingertips. From there, my mind plays a torturous game of *What other parts of her body are hot?* Her breasts? Her thighs? Her—

"I can feel your boner poking against my back, by the way." The chair's backrest leaves a gap between her lower back and shoulders, and she wiggles her tailbone against my growing erection.

"So?" I drawl.

"So it's not appropriate."

I roll my eyes, wondering what she'd say if she knew I wasn't wearing anything under my jeans. Tomorrow I'll need to buy some new clothes, but until then I'm going commando.

Actually, she probably wouldn't even blink if she knew that. Why would she? This chick is neither easily affected nor impressed.

Christ. How is it possible that the one woman who's intrigued me in a long time is also the one woman who wants nothing to do with me? The chemistry between us is combustible, but apparently chemistry doesn't impress Maggie Reilly either. We haven't even had sex and already she's shooing me off the stage.

But being the seasoned performer that I am, I have no intention of being shooed away.

Instead, I taunt her. "Don't act like you're not getting wet feeling me against you."

"Wet? No. But I am a little hungry. Should we order a pizza?"

Some primitive part of me makes me swivel the chair, determined to prove to this woman that my aroused state turns her on. Maggie's eyes widen as I sink to my knees and rest my hands on her hips. My fingers toy with the waistband of her black yoga pants.

"What are you doing?" She practically squeaks out the question. "I told you I have work to do."

"And I told you it's time to take a break."

"You don't get to dictate—"

"Orgasm," I interrupt.

She blinks. "What?"

"Do you want an orgasm?"

Exasperation fills her eyes. "Do you always talk in riddles?"

"Who's riddling? I'm asking you a question—are you in the

71

mood for an orgasm?" I lick my bottom lip. "Because I'm in the mood to give you one."

Her lips part slightly. Then her mouth falls entirely open.

Grinning at her reaction, I gently lift her ass off the chair so I can peel her pants off her legs. She doesn't stop me. In fact, her breathing quickens as my palms slide over each smooth inch of skin that is revealed.

"You don't need to wax your legs," I accuse as I toss the yoga pants aside.

She sighs. "I know. I lied."

My mouth lifts in another grin, partly because of her admission, partly because the agitated look on her face is completely foreign on her. Since I've met her, she's been cool and composed, even when her green eyes flash with anger, when her cheeks redden with arousal. I like it all, but not as much as I enjoy the naked vulnerability and raw desire on her face right now.

Maybe it's the challenge, or maybe it's infatuation, or maybe she simply represents some level of normalcy that's been missing from my life since I became famous. Whatever the reason, I can't help myself from trying to seduce her. I continue to stroke her legs, and then move my hands north again. Touching the damp crotch of her bright yellow panties, I fight a chuckle. "Told you you're wet."

"You're imagining it."

I drag my fingers up to her waistband.

She groans and tries to wriggle away from my caress. "I don't have time for this," she grumbles.

"Sure you do."

"I have homework..."

My hands still, because I'm not about to keep going without her consent. I meet her eyes, my tone serious. "If you say the word *stop*, I'll stop. If you say the word *no*, I'll stop. But you haven't said either of those words." I flick up a brow. "So are you saying yes?"

After an interminable long beat, she dips her head in a nod and whispers, "Yes."

Without another word, I remove her panties and toss them aside. Then I lower my head and place a soft kiss on her clit.

She gasps.

Then sighs.

Then moans.

Fighting back a smile, I kiss her again, and again, and again, until it dawns on me that I'm not out to prove a point anymore. I intended to show her she can't hide the effect I have on her and prove the attraction between us is mutual. But as I run my tongue over her slick pussy, I forget about all that.

She tastes like heaven. I swirl lazy figure-eights over her clit, savoring the sweet taste of her, groaning against her when she releases a whimper of pleasure and widens her legs. If my cock wasn't throbbing relentlessly and my head wasn't buzzing with lust, I might've been able to maintain the slow pace.

But I'm painfully, desperately aroused, and all I can do is speed up, suddenly anxious to bring her over the edge and make her scream my name as she comes.

The wish is fulfilled a lot faster than I expected. All it takes is for me to slide one finger deep inside her pussy and suck her clit hard in my mouth, and she shudders with an orgasm so powerful I almost come in my pants.

Maggie isn't one of those chicks who bites her lip and writhes in silent pleasure. Oh no. She vocalizes every sexy second of her climax. Moaning. Trembling. As the words "Oh *fuck*" gasp out of her mouth, she tangles her fingers in my hair and locks her thighs around my head.

When she finally whimpers and grows still, I pull back, a

satisfied grin on my face and an unsatisfied erection straining against my zipper.

"You don't play fair," Maggie murmurs, cheeks flushed, eyes a little glazed.

"Never have," I say easily. I give her inner thigh a light pinch and hop to my feet. Her disheveled appearance sparks a rush of satisfaction, because I know I'm responsible for it. "All right, Red. Good hustle. I'm hopping into the shower now." I offer a gracious smile. "You can go ahead and finish your homework."

14

MAGGIE

*H*e wants to play games? Is that it? I gape at Ben's sexy backside as he disappears into the hallway.

What the hell was that? I inhale a deep breath, then stumble off the chair and bend down to retrieve my panties from the floor. I'm still a little stunned by what happened, and more than a little shaky from the exquisite orgasm that just rocked my world.

Ben Barrett made me come in a record-breaking three minutes. He hadn't asked me what I liked. Hadn't waited for me to guide him. He simply knew. It doesn't surprise me. The second I slid into bed with him two nights ago I knew this man possessed the ability to set my body on fire. And he fully took advantage of that ability just now, effectively ensuring that I'd never be able to concentrate on schoolwork now.

It's hard to stand when my core still throbs from Ben's orgasmic treatment, but I force myself to my feet. I walk toward the bathroom on wobbly legs, my determination deepening when I hear the shower running.

If he wants to play games, I'm ready to play back. If only to give my aroused body what it wants so I can finish researching my paper without any distractions.

At least that's what I tell myself as I turn the doorknob and step into the small, steam-filled bathroom. The pink plastic curtain shields Ben from my view, and me from his.

"Are you joining me or what?" His muffled voice breaks through the sound of water flowing.

My nostrils flare. Damn it. I don't even have the element of surprise on my side. How did he know I'd follow him in here? Is he so arrogant that he just assumed I'd run into the bathroom to get a glimpse of his naked body?

It's what you did, isn't it?

I push the annoying reminder out of my head and reach for the edge of the shower curtain. As I pull it open, a billow of steam clouds my vision. When it clears, my eyes focus, and the sight of Ben, wet, hard and naked, is enough to suck all the oxygen out of my lungs.

My brain goes into overload trying to absorb all the delicious little details. Like his smooth, golden skin. And his rippled abs. And his firm, muscular thighs. And his...oh, gosh, his everything.

"You're letting the cold air in," he complains.

I swallow, trying to regain my composure. Then I slip my shirt over my head, let it drop to the floor, and step into the shower. The second I do, Ben plants his hands on my bare hips. He pulls me into the stream of water and captures my lips with his.

Hoo-boy. He gives me another one of those rough, drugging kisses, but this time I break lip contact before I can completely lose myself in his kiss.

I lean on my tiptoes and press my lips to his ear so he can hear me over the rush of water. "I don't like being interrupted from my work," I say mockingly.

He raises his brow, sending droplets down his aristocratic nose and into the thick stubble on his chin. "Okay. Should I apologize for making you come?"

"No." I run my hand over his wet chest. One flat, brown nipple hardens beneath my fingers. "I'm just voicing my disapproval."

"So, what, you crashed my shower to punish me?" One side of his mouth lifts in a crooked grin. His metallic blue eyes smolder when he says the word *punish*.

"Something like that."

I glide my hand down his chest and encircle his shaft.

He inhales sharply, eyes narrowing with arousal. Water droplets pool over his upper lip. Feeling bold, I lean forward and lick the moisture off. Then I meet his gaze and offer a crooked grin of my own, before sinking to my knees and taking his cock in my mouth.

This time his jagged intake of breath is followed by a low groan. His hands tangle in my hair, which has matted against my forehead. I push a few wet strands out of my eyes and lick him from base to tip, enjoying his masculine taste.

And unlike Ben, I take my time teasing him. I drag my lips over his tip, sucking, kissing, stroking his balls with my palm. I torture him with long strokes of my tongue and pull back each time he tries to thrust deeper.

His husky moans and the feel of the hot water streaming over my breasts drives me crazy. I clamp my knees together and try to focus on bringing him to the edge, until he tugs at my hair and I look up to meet his heavy-lidded gaze.

"Touch yourself," he orders, his words hissing through the steam filling the small space. "I want to see you play with yourself."

I swallow back a whimper and nod. Widening my knees, I press my fingers between my legs and take him in my mouth again. Going slow is no longer an option, not when I can feel Ben watching me as I rub my clit, not when I can feel his thick cock pulsing against my tongue.

We come together, hard, fast. He fills my mouth and I swallow every last drop, while my own orgasm sizzles my nerve endings in a wave of pleasure that numbs every part of my body.

With a ragged groan, Ben gently pushes my head back and sinks to the floor of the tub, looking completely and thoroughly spent. He reaches out and brushes hair out of my eyes, then strokes one of my trembling thighs. "You okay?"

I know I must look like a drowned rat, still shaking from the climax and gasping for air, and I laugh at the concern I see in his eyes. "I'm fine. Numb, but fine."

He grins. "In case you're wondering, I'm fine too."

I glance at his crotch. He's still sporting an erection, and I'm shocked to feel my nipples harden with desire. Ugh, I hate this guy. How is he still hard? And how am I, the person who just experienced my second orgasm in twenty minutes, ready to go *again*?

I'm not sure what makes me jump to my feet, that startling realization or the sudden change of water temperature, which goes from lukewarm to lukecold. Whatever the reason, I quickly tug on the shower curtain and stumble onto the fluffy pink bathroom mat.

Ben calls my name, but I ignore him.

Two days, I realize as I wrap a bathrobe around my wet body and hurry out of the room. Two days since I'd first met Ben Barrett, two days of allowing him to distract me to no end, and now two orgasms that still haven't managed to flush the man from my system.

What's the matter with me?

"What's the matter with you?" Ben sounds out of breath

and annoyed as he marches into my bedroom wearing nothing but a towel.

I tighten the sash of the robe and cross my arms over the thick terrycloth. "Nothing is the matter."

"So you always sprint out of a room after sex?"

"We didn't have sex."

Laughter spurts from his throat. "We came pretty damn close. In fact, we came pretty damn hard."

My cheeks burn. "But we didn't cross the line."

A shadow floats across his face. "I wasn't even aware there was a line."

"Well, there is."

I feel unbearably exposed, standing there in my bathrobe, the hardwood floor icy under my bare feet. And unbelievably confused, because my mouth keeps saying words that make Ben frown and my body keeps berating me for it.

"So this line..." His frown turns into a scowl. "Is it the one that keeps you from having fun?"

"What?"

"You heard me. You crossed over from uptight land to fun world, and now you're trying to convince yourself what we did was wrong."

He's right—I *am* trying to convince myself we've done something wrong. But it has nothing to do with being uptight and everything to do with the way he makes me feel. Tony and I have done things in bed that nobody would ever consider uptight, but not once have I lost my head over Tony. Not once did I choose Tony over studying or finishing an essay.

I've seen what happens when you let yourself get sidetracked by a man. Hell, my own mother abandoned me because of a man. But I'm not going to be that stupid. I'm not going to abandon the path I've set for myself, or desert my goals and my dreams for some guy. Even one who makes my entire body tremble from one penetrating gaze.

"You think I'm uptight?" I decide to respond to the one remark he'd made that didn't hit close to home.

"Yep." He leans one bare shoulder against the doorframe and casts a glare in my direction. "You're anti-fun, Red."

Irritation prickles at me. "No, I'm not. I simply have different priorities than you."

"What's that supposed to mean?"

"It means my life doesn't revolve around fun. I have a job, I have goals, I have responsibilities. Unlike you, I don't have time to gallivant around or spend a whole day in bed, not if I want to pay my bills." My jaw tightens. "I'm not as lucky as you, Ben. Twenty million dollars doesn't just fall out of the sky and into my lap."

He makes an exasperated sound. "I wasn't asking you to quit your job, Maggie. Only to let loose and enjoy your day off."

"Sorry, but I don't have that luxury. In my life there's no such thing as a day off."

Shaking his head, he edges away from the doorway. "Wow. Sounds like you lead a mighty fulfilling life," he cracks before disappearing into the hall.

"Ben," I call after him.

His footsteps stop. "Yeah?"

I sigh. "You should probably look for a hotel."

*a*fter I've gotten dressed and brushed my hair, I enter the living room to find it empty. The only signs of life come from the television Ben left on. Some entertainment show silently flashes across the screen.

He left without saying goodbye.

It shouldn't bother me, but it does.

"You're the one who told him to find a hotel," I mutter to myself. I collapse on the couch, stretching out my legs to rest my feet on the coffee table.

Right about now, every female in America would be screaming vile things at me if they knew I sent Ben Barrett away. But to hell with them. I'm too busy to be playing hookup games with some egomaniac celebrity. I have way more important things to do.

Growing up, I never felt like I belonged. At school, I was a loner. At home, I was invisible. I was passed up for adoption so many times I'd given up on ever finding someone who truly cared about me. It was like being the last person picked for a game of softball. Standing there as everyone around you got picked one by one, feeling humiliated and unloved, as useless as a piece of trash on the sidewalk. Only the stakes were higher than a silly sports game. It was about a child not being good enough to have parents.

It wasn't until I started studying social work and working with kids that I finally found a place where I fit in. I found my identity at the youth center. It's where I developed this hunger to help kids and ensure they grow up feeling like they matter. It took me years to get past the pain and resentment of being abandoned—I don't want any of the kids I work with to ever feel as alone as I have.

So what if it means putting relationships on hold for a while? I won't be single forever, just until I graduate and find a good job. Then I'll go out and do what other women my age do. I'll date and flirt and maybe even get married. Other Ben Barretts will come along. It isn't like saying goodbye to this one will have life-altering effects—

"The ladies love Ben Barrett!"

I yelp when a cheerful female voice breaks through the dismal silence in the room. Shifting, I feel the remote control dig into my butt and realize I accidentally pressed un-mute when I moved my legs.

I yank the remote from under me but can't bring myself to shut off the TV. Not when Ben's ridiculously sexy face mocks me from the screen. It's like driving past a gory car crash. You just can't look away.

"Bad boy Barrett might be stirring up some scandals recently, but the *Heart of a Hero* star still manages to stir up the ladies."

No kidding.

"Shanika Thomas, our New York correspondent, spent the day in the Big Apple chatting with Barrett's fans, who don't seem to mind all the negative attention their favorite action hero is receiving. In fact, it's unanimous—we all love him."

"Oh my God, Ben is sooooo cute!" a fan giggles into Shanika Thomas' microphone. "I don't care if he, like, slept with a married woman. He's still hot!"

"I'm a married woman and he can sure sleep with me," another fan remarks with a laugh. She lowers her voice. "Just don't tell my husband I said that."

"I don't know who his new girlfriend is," someone else sighs. "But I'd go to a hotel with Ben Barrett any night of the week!"

"Well, there you have it," Shanika chirps into the mic. "Scandalous or not, it looks like Ben continues to scandalize the hearts of his fans."

Scandalize the hearts? What does that even mean?

Rolling my eyes, I shut off the TV. A second later, I hear the front door swing open.

I hop off the couch, startled, then relax slightly when Ben enters the apartment. "Oh," I blurt out. "You're still here?"

"Sure am."

He strides toward me, dropping a set of keys—*my* keys—on the hall table before approaching the living area. He holds a large paper bag with splotches of grease at the bottom of and steam rising from the top.

"I went out and got us some Chinese food. I don't like pizza all that much."

"But..."

"You asked me to leave?" He cocks a brow. "That's not going to happen, Mags."

I bristle at his use of the nickname. "Why not?"

"Because you like me. And I happen to like you."

"I also like Joe the hot dog vendor. Doesn't mean I'm going to let him move in with me and turn my life upside down."

"Who said anything about moving in with you?" He flops down on the couch, sets the bag on the coffee table and shoots me a look that says *you don't understand me at all.*

Um, I *don't* understand him. He's Ben Barrett, for God's sake. After watching a two-minute TV segment on him, I'm pretty sure he could walk out of here and have five phone numbers in his pocket before he even leaves the building.

So why the hell is he still here?

"All I want to do is spend some time with you," he adds. "And if you're honest, you'll admit you want to spend time with me."

"Ben—"

He silences me by raising a hand, and like an obedient third-grader, my jaw slams shut.

"I have a proposition for you," he announces, a grin tugging on one side of his mouth.

Wariness circles me. "What kind of proposition?"

"I'll have sex with you if you let me stay here a while."

Wait. *What?*

With a pleasant expression, he begins removing items from the take-out bag. He carefully places each cardboard container on the table. He reaches into the bag for the napkins and cutlery.

I stare at him.

Obviously I misheard him, because no way did he just offer to *sleep with me* in exchange for room and board.

Yeah... I'm not even humoring this one.

I shift my suspicions to the feast he's laying out on the table. I told him to check into a hotel, and instead he's come back with that cocky attitude and a bag of Chinese food that smells so damn good and makes my empty stomach growl in anticipation.

"Gimme that," I grumble, grabbing the carton of egg rolls from his hands.

"That's all you've got to say?" Ben watches as I munch on a roll, his eyes bewildered. "You're not going to respond to my proposition?"

I spare him a withering glance. "No."

"Why the fuck not?"

"Because it's so ridiculous it doesn't merit a response."

"It's not ridiculous and you know it."

"What I know," I say, swallowing before reaching for another egg roll, "is that you're nuts. I'm not giving you a place to stay in exchange for sex."

"Why not? We both know you really need the sex."

My nostrils flare. Deciding it's best to ignore this entire absurd exchange, I reach for a carton of chicken fried rice and grab a fork.

My silent treatment seems to work, because Ben closes his mouth. But he continues to watch me, so intently, so knowingly, that it becomes increasingly difficult to ignore the flicker of heat in my belly.

Fine, so maybe his proposition isn't *totally* ridiculous. Maybe the thought of having sex with Ben is even more delicious than this food. Maybe giving him a blowjob in the shower had been one of the hottest sexual experiences of my life and maybe I want to do it again.

Doesn't mean I'll give in.

"How long is your roommate away for?" he finally asks.

"Eight days." I chew slowly. "Not that it should matter to you. You're not staying here."

He leans back against the sofa cushions. "You don't find my offer the least bit tempting?"

"Nope."

"Liar."

I ignore the jab and dig into a plate of vegetables, hoping he'll just drop this.

But that's hoping for too much, of course.

Before I can blink, he swipes the fork from my hands and

tosses it on the table. Then, without giving me time to protest, he pulls me onto his lap and grasps my hips so I can't move.

"Let me stay with you, Maggie."

"No," I say, trying very hard to ignore the warmth of his hands against my hips, the heat of his groin against my thighs.

He dips his head and brushes a soft kiss over my lips. My attempt at moving away is futile. He just moves one hand to the back of my head and threads his fingers through my hair, holding me in place.

"Let me stay with you," he whispers against my mouth. Then he licks my lower lip. Captures it with his teeth and starts nibbling.

I give an involuntary moan.

Grinning, he pulls back. "C'mon," he coaxes. "You know you don't want me to leave."

An argument reaches my lips, but when I open my mouth, nothing comes out.

"You came to that hotel because you needed a release. I can give you that release."

I shift, trying to ease off his lap, but all I succeed in doing is rubbing against his dick, which hardens instantly.

"Forget about Tony. I'll give you all the sex you crave and more."

My cheeks grow pink and finally I find my voice. "I'm not some virgin you need to deflower."

"I don't want to deflower you. I want to fuck you." His voice takes on a seductive note. "Eight days. For the next eight days I'll fuck your brains out. Anything you want me to do to you, I'll do. Anytime you want it, you'll have it."

Oh God. His words send a bolt of desire down my spine and straight to my pussy. I've already come twice today, but suddenly I'm aching for release again. How does he manage to do this to me, to send me into a state of mindless lust?

"And all you have to do in return," Ben finishes, "is hang out with me for a while and let me crash here. The way I see it"—his tongue darts out and drags along my bottom lip—"you definitely get the better end of the deal, babe."

"You don't play fair," I accuse.

"Like I said, never have." He slides his hands underneath my shirt and cups my bare boobs.

A jolt of pleasure torpedoes into me.

"So, what'll it be? All you've gotta do is give me a place to stay and you have your very own boy toy," he teases. "You know it's a damn good deal."

I almost purr as he strokes my breasts and then tweaks my nipples playfully. It's hard to think with his hands on my tits, but for the life of me, I can't shrug them away. They feel too good against my flushed skin, the feel of his hard cock between my legs too damn tantalizing.

"Ground rules," I manage to choke out.

The words surprise me. Ground rules? Am I actually agreeing to this?

Ben sighs. "Let's hear them."

"You don't interfere with my job," I say firmly. "And you don't interrupt me when I'm studying."

"Done. Is that it?" He lightly pinches one nipple with his fingers, and I gasp in delight. Damn him. Doesn't he know that by doing that to me he's turning my brain into mush? From the faint grin on his face, he definitely knows.

I make a frantic attempt to think of more rules, but none come to mind. Dammit. This is way too easy—for him. All he had to do was dangle the sex carrot under my nose and I was ready to take a bite out of it. There should've been a dozen reasons why letting Ben stay with me is a bad, bad idea, but somehow all those reasons elude me. It doesn't help that he's still fondling my breasts, and it definitely doesn't help that my panties are completely soaked.

"Maggie?" he prompts.

His hands are still under my shirt, his fingers still caressing my painfully hard nipples. His erection remains pressed against my unbelievably wet pussy, and I'm no longer able to concentrate on anything but those sensations.

I suck in a breath and say, "Eight days, Barrett. Don't complicate my life."

"And the sex?"

I exhale in a rush. "You just said—anything I want, anytime I want it." My fingers curl over his impossibly broad shoulders. "Well, I want it now."

16

BEN

*W*ithout a word, I follow Maggie down the hall. She steps into the bathroom, then returns with a box of condoms in her hands, and I'm barely able to conceal my smile of satisfaction. Oh yeah. Not only have I managed to secure myself a place to stay away from the prying eyes of the press, I actually convinced Maggie to go to bed with me. Not an easy feat, considering she's obviously a workaholic who views sex as a complication.

Fortunately, I am here to fix that.

We reach her bedroom. I stand in the doorway for a second, the smile finally reaching my lips when Maggie flops down on the bed and lies on her back. She's wearing a loose cotton tank top and a pair of yoga pants, hardly an outfit that screams seduction, but something about the casual attire turns me on. I like that she doesn't go to great lengths to doll herself up. The way she dresses reflects the no-nonsense attitude I get from her.

"Come here," she orders, though her voice is equally throaty and apprehensive.

I step closer. "Should my clothes stay on or come off?"

"What kind of question is that? What do *you* think?"

Chuckling, I grip the hem of my T-shirt and then pull the material over my head.

Maggie's eyes widen at the sight of my bare chest, and my cock jerks in response. No matter how annoying she claims to find me, she can't deny her attraction and we both know it.

Unzipping my jeans, I slide them off and kick them aside. My cock happily springs up.

Her breath hitches. "No boxers?"

"I need to go shopping for clothes tomorrow."

"You don't need clothes. You're much more attractive naked."

I hold my hand to my heart and shoot her a mock smile. "Aw baby, was that a compliment?"

"Unfortunately." She sighs dramatically. "I should've known better. Your ego's big enough already."

Buck-naked I approach the bed, frowning when she makes no move to undress. "Take off your clothes," I command. "I feel at a disadvantage."

"Take them off for me. You're the boy toy, remember?" She gives a mischievous grin. "Besides, if you want to stay here, you need to earn the room and board."

I can't stop another chuckle. I like sassy women. I like this one in particular, but I suspect that's because she isn't deliberately trying to be sassy. She simply is.

"C'mon, Mr. Movie Star. Let's see what you've got," she taunts.

My eyes narrow. "Is that a challenge?"

"Yep. And at the moment you're definitely not meeting it."

I sit down on the edge of the bed. "You realize you won't be this smug when I'm through with you?"

Before she can answer, I lean forward and grasp the waistband of her pants. Slowly, I roll the material down her smooth legs, brushing my fingertips along every inch of skin that

I reveal. I hear her breath hitch again and fight a smile. No matter how much she pretends to be in control, I know that all it'll take is one touch, one lick to her pussy, and she'll be a moaning, trembling mess.

I throw her pants on the floor before focusing my attention on her tank top. Instead of removing it, I stretch out beside her and kiss her breasts through the shirt. The kiss leaves a wet spot on the material and causes both her nipples to pucker eagerly.

"Let's get this off," she says, fumbling for the hem of her top.

"No."

I grab both her hands with one of mine and shove her wrists over her head, clasping them with my fingers. Dipping my head again, I rub my mouth over her covered tits, then bite one of her nipples. She flinches, but I know I haven't hurt her. The glazed look in her eyes tells me she's enjoying every second of this. I continue to nibble, my tongue pulsing with the need to slide underneath the thin shirt and taste her skin. But not yet.

Not until she begs for it.

Maybe it makes me a pompous ass, but I want this woman to beg. She might've agreed to let me stay at her place, and to hop into bed with me, but she'd acted almost like she was doing me a favor, and I'm desperate to prove to her that our attraction goes both ways. That she wants me just as badly as I want her.

Still holding her wrists against the headboard, I slide my free hand up her body and cup one perky breast. I squeeze, enjoying the little whimper of distress she gives. Nearly a full minute ticks by, but still I make no move to rip off her shirt, instead teasing her tits and kissing her nipples until she squirms beneath me.

"Please," she finally begs.

I poke my tongue in my cheek and lift my head to meet her agitated green eyes. "Please what?"

"Please take my shirt off."

"Anything else?" I ask mockingly.

I see the cloud of desire and irritation on her face, and I know it's hard for her to admit how badly she wants this. *Needs* this. She surprises me, though. With a strangled groan, she sucks in a long breath, then says, "Fuck me, Ben. Please."

It's all I need to hear.

With a groan of my own, I tear the tank top off her body and press my mouth to her delectable tits, feasting on each one. I don't think I'll ever get my fill, but the heat of her pussy against my hip is too hard to ignore.

Sucking one nipple deep in my mouth, I hook my thumb under the waistband of her panties and push them down. I cup her, moaning when her juices coat my palm.

"You're so fucking wet," I croak.

She makes a grumbling sound. "You seem to make that happen. A lot."

I bristle at her forlorn tone. "Don't act like you don't love how wet I make you."

To prove my point, I shove one finger inside her pussy, and it's instantly surrounded by heat and moisture. My mouth tingles, aching with the need to taste this girl again. Releasing her wrists, I plant one last kiss to her breasts and then slide down her body until my head is positioned between her thighs.

"Fuck," I mutter. "I'm dying to put my mouth on you again."

"Then do it," she whispers.

My tongue travels along one firm thigh, licking her smooth skin before gliding toward her clit. Her soft moans drive me wild, light my entire body on fire, but I manage to hold on to my restraint. Maggie gives a breathy whimper as I flick the tip of my tongue over her swollen clit, and when I begin to suck on it, she shudders. I lift my head, grinning at the desperate heat flashing in her eyes. Pleased with her reaction, I continue to explore her sweet pussy, enjoying the way she arches her hips to allow me greater access. I add a second finger into the mix and begin a lazy rhythm that causes another moan to escape her lips. When her hands start clawing at the sheets, I finally quicken the pace, suck hard on her clit, and she promptly topples over the edge.

She comes hard, and just listening to her hoarse moans and feeling the orgasm vibrate through her body makes my cock twitch with anticipation.

I give her some time to recover, my head resting on her thigh, my heart pounding like a jackhammer. When she goes still, I slide my way up her body and kiss her hard, but she quickly wiggles out from under me and pushes me onto my back.

"My turn," Maggie says, a hazy glow in her eyes.

"Didn't you just have your turn?" I mock.

"Just shut up and enjoy this."

My blood surges as her fingertips graze my neck, and my pulse speeds up when I notice the wicked gleam in her eyes. The memory of what she did to me in the shower earlier, with her lips and tongue and hands, floats into my head and my dick begins to ache. I'm so turned on I don't think I can handle another blowjob, no matter how incredible it is. I won't last long at all, and I still want to fuck her.

"Don't worry, I'll stop before you come," she mocks back, as if she's read my mind.

A second later her mouth clamps down on my neck. She sucks on it, the pressure of her lips causing a shiver to sizzle down my spine and grab hold of my balls. Closing my eyes, I lose myself to sensation, to the feel of Maggie's lips trailing wet kisses along my flesh. Her mouth travels toward to my chest, where she nibbles on one flat nipple, then down to my abdomen, where she licks the line of hair leading down to my crotch. When she finally reaches my cock, I'm harder than ever and so close to exploding I can barely move.

One lick, one light kiss to my pre-come-soaked tip, is all I'm willing to allow. Any more and I'll be shooting my load in her mouth, when all I want to do is bury my cock inside her.

Laughing quietly, she puts me out of my misery and climbs back up, straddling me with her long legs. "You're close, aren't you?" She leans toward the nightstand and reaches for the condom box.

"What the hell do you think?" I growl. My cock twitches as she covers it with a condom.

"Pity. I expect my boy toys to possess stamina," she says with mock disapproval.

Before I can offer a comeback, she sucks the breath right out of my lungs by impaling herself onto my dick. White-hot pleasure slices into me like a knife.

"*Jesus,*" I grunt.

"Still close?" she teases.

I manage a nod. Shit. I'm impossibly turned on, and dangerously close.

I rise up in an attempt to kiss her, but she shifts her head so my lips connect with her cheek, and makes a tsking sound. "None of that," she chides. "I'm still having my way with you."

Then she presses her mouth to my jaw, planting barely-there kisses. She grinds her lower body against mine but doesn't ride me the way I want her to. When I make another attempt to kiss her, she allows it, but this time her tongue is in charge, exploring my mouth with precision.

I groan, the guttural sound filling the bedroom.

Maggie breaks the kiss with a faint grin. "You know," she muses, "I recall you telling me I wouldn't be so smug once you had your way with me...and yet I'm still feeling smug."

"Yeah, what about now?" Without giving her time to react, I dig my fingers into her hips and thrust upwards, driving my cock deeper inside her.

She gasps, her eyes wide with pleasure and surprise. "Now...I'm feeling less smug," she admits, then cries out when I give another hard thrust.

"And now?"

"Now...I'm...um..." Her expression glazes over as she struggles to speak.

I thrust again.

"And now?"

She gives a breathy moan. "Now I just want to fuck you."

And she does. She rides me so hard I can barely see straight, her pussy clamped so tightly around my dick that I'm mindless with intense pleasure bordering on blissful pain. I lock my gaze to hers and watch as her expression changes from needy to satisfied, and then she's coming again, her inner muscles squeezing my cock and triggering a climax that turns my vision into a mist.

Maggie collapses on top of me, her breasts crushed against my damp chest, her breathing ragged. After a moment she moves off and lies flat on her back, those gorgeous tits rising and falling with each breath. I stay quiet, trying to control my own breathing, trying to recover from the body-numbing release.

"So...anytime I want it?" she asks, and her voice is a bit wheezy

I find myself laughing. "That's what I promised, didn't I?"

"Good." She rolls over, presses her cheek against my chest and promptly falls asleep in my arms.

17

BEN

*I*t only takes three days for me to realize that Maggie Reilly needs a lot more than sex. She needs a goddamn vacation.

I honestly can't understand how she lives the way she does. Her life revolves around work and school, and while I admire her self-discipline, it's almost superhuman. She spends the mornings studying and writing papers, and the afternoons at the community center where she volunteers. Then she comes home and buries her nose in a textbook for a couple more hours. By the evening, she's getting ready to go to work, where she spends the night waiting tables. She returns around two a.m. and goes straight to bed. She eats only when I force her to, and shoots down my suggestions that she take a walk or watch Netflix with me. In fact, the only time she actually seems grateful for my company is when we're in bed together.

She's more interested in my body than in my attempts for us to get to know each other. Don't get me wrong, I'm not complaining about the sex—if anything, it only gets better each time we get naked. But it bugs me that Maggie doesn't make any time for herself, and it's becoming unsettlingly obvious that Maggie needs more than sex. She needs fun. Relaxation. A *life*.

I don't think the words *relax* or *unwind* are even in her vocabulary. And as an objective observer, I grow more and more troubled each time I find her asleep at the computer desk and have to carry her to bed at four in the morning.

Not that I don't appreciate a solid work ethic, because I do. Despite what Maggie thinks, I worked hard for the money sitting in my bank account, the money I earned before Gretchen shocked me and the world by leaving me a part of her fortune. Acting isn't all fun and games, and when I'm in the middle of an intense shoot, I barely leave my house, let alone socialize.

But in all the years I've been doing this, I've always forced myself to take breaks, to make sure my work doesn't monopolize my life. I've seen a fair amount of actors crash and burn, make six films back to back and get so lost in the industry they didn't even know who they were anymore.

Maggie might not be in the movie business, but she's a workaholic through and through. She needs to slow down, and I've officially dubbed myself the man who'll help her do that.

It's time to step in. I promised her I wouldn't complicate her life, but this is just plain ridiculous. As much as I love having a quiet place to hide out, how much longer can I really watch Maggie waste her life away?

At the moment, she's on the other end of the couch, devouring a book about autism. She hasn't gotten up in three hours. I want to suggest we order a pizza or something, but I know trying to get her to quit when she's still absorbed in her work will get me nowhere.

Instead, I flick on the TV, instantly groaning when I see what's on.

For the first time all afternoon, Maggie glances up from her book. Her gaze follows mine and she makes a face when she sees the entertainment segment. "Don't these people have lives?" she grumbles.

I turn up the volume.

"Ben Barrett's newest flame must be keeping him very busy," the host says with a mischievous grin. "The sexy action star has been off the radar for nearly a week now and everyone is wondering how he's been passing the time..."

"Should we tell them?" Maggie says with a tiny grin.

"Was that an honest-to-God joke?" I return with mock-amazement. "Holy shit. I didn't think you were capable of anything but working."

"Ha ha."

"Early in the week, Barrett's car was found vandalized in front of a New York City strip club," the host continues. "It was later revealed he spent the night in a hotel with an unidentified woman..."

"They make you sound like a sleazebag," Maggie says.

"Although rumors are swirling that Barrett is out of sight due to a secret elopement with his mysterious new flame—"

A burst of laughter rings out, courtesy of Maggie.

"—a source close to the actor admits that Barrett is keeping a low profile because of the Gretchen Goodrich scandal. Goodrich, who was the wife of Academy-Award-winning director Alan Goodrich, recently left Barrett a sizable fortune after—"

I turn off the TV with an angry frown. Damn vultures. Why the fuck can't they just leave me alone? Why can't they let Gretchen rest in peace?

"So..." Maggie's curious voice breaks through my thoughts. "Are you ever going to tell me what happened with Gretchen Goodrich?"

"Sure." I turn my head and stare her down. "If you agree to take a break for a couple of days."

"I don't take breaks."

"Then start."

She rolls her eyes. "We've been through this already."

"I don't care. I don't think it's healthy that you bury yourself in work and school."

"Good thing it doesn't matter what you think. It's my life, Ben."

"Yeah. Sure. It's your life." I hop to my feet, unable to stop a scowl from creasing my mouth. "I'm taking a shower. I'd ask you to join me, but you've still got, what, three hundred more pages to read?" I gaze pointedly at the textbook in her lap before striding out of the living room.

She doesn't follow me, and I didn't expect her to. The past three days have taught me that Maggie shuts down the moment I criticize her lifestyle.

I enter the bathroom and rip off my T-shirt and jeans before stepping into the shower stall. As the warm water slides down my body, I dunk my head under the spray and release a frustrated groan. Why am I letting Maggie's workaholic bullshit get to me, anyway? So what if she hardly goes out? That TV piece we just saw confirms that the media storm surrounding me is still going strong, which means I definitely need to stay out of sight for a while longer. Holing up here with Maggie is the perfect solution.

I've never been one to duck and hide when troubles arise, but these past few days have reminded me of what life before fame had been like. It brings back memories of growing up in Ohio, of being able to take a girl out without it winding up in the tabloids, of being able to sing along to the Beach Boys without a sound bite popping up on the Internet. I want to hold on to this unburdened feeling for as long as I can, to think about someone other than myself for a while. I don't know where it is all heading, but for the moment I need to be around her. Need that feeling of being a regular person.

But it pisses me off to see her driving herself to the point of exhaustion. I like her. Fuck, I like her a lot. And what I don't like is seeing someone I like wasting her life away. I feel compelled to do something, but how the hell can I break down Maggie's impenetrable devotion to her job and her annoying tendency to choose responsibility over fun?

I stand in the shower for a moment, letting the water course down my body, and then the answer comes to me.

With a grin, I shut off the water and step onto the fluffy pink bathmat. I wrap a towel around my waist and head for Maggie's bedroom, where I sit at the edge of the bed and do a quick search on my phone. Once I find the number, I glance over to make sure I closed the door and then dial.

"The Olive Martini. Trisha speaking."

"Trisha, hey." I lower my voice, check the door again, and say, "I'm calling about Maggie Reilly."

"Who is this?" The voice on the other end thickens with suspicion.

I falter for a moment before responding with, "My name's Tony, and—"

"Tony? Oh my God! I didn't recognize your voice."

Shit. I hadn't banked on any of the other wait staff knowing the infamous Tony.

"Uh, I'm trying to speak quietly. Maggie's in the other room and I don't want her to overhear."

"Oh. Okay. Well, how are you doing? What's up?"

"I'm doing great, Trish." I really hope Tony calls her *Trish*. Sounds like a Tony thing to do. "How's life treating ya?"

"Can't complain. Actually, I'm lying. Life would be a lot better if I wasn't spending my Friday night serving a bunch of rude theater snobs."

I chuckle. "Doesn't sound like fun," I agree. "Anyway, the reason I'm calling is—"

"You said it was about Maggie?"

"It is." I send another covert look to the door. "Trish. I need you to do me a really big favor..."

18

MAGGIE

"I want to take you on a trip."

My head snaps up, not so much from Ben's sudden reappearance but because of his random declaration. He approaches the couch, clad in a pair of jeans and a navy-blue long-sleeved shirt, his hair still damp from the shower. His jaw is tight and his mouth is set in a firm line, as if he came out here expecting a fight and is prepared to win it.

His words hang in the air. A trip? Hadn't he listened to a word I said ten minutes ago?

"I don't have time to take—"

"I'm not talking a week-long vacation," he interrupts, catching the disbelief in my eyes. "I'm talking one night. Well, two, since we'd leave tonight and come back Saturday morning."

"I'm working tomorrow."

"So call in sick." He offers a small shrug. "C'mon, babe, it's just one shift."

My jaw tenses at his flippant tone. "I can't lie to my manager about being sick. That's bad karma."

"Maggie."

"Ben."

ELLE KENNEDY

I don't like the way he's looking at me. The secretive smile playing on his sexy lips tells me he's up to something.

Before I can further analyze his sly expression, my phone rings. Grateful for the interruption, I lean over and grab it from the coffee table. Trisha's name flashes on the screen, along with two new voicemails alerts. I'd turned off the ringer earlier because three irritating telemarketers had called one after the other.

"Hello?" I avoid eye contact with Ben as I press the phone to my ear.

"Hey, it's me."

Since Trisha rarely calls me, my guard instantly shoots up a few feet. "What's up, Trish?"

"I need a favor—could you switch shifts with me? I'll work for you tomorrow night if you do Saturday."

Something is fishy, all right.

My head swivels in Ben's direction, but he seems completely uninterested in my conversation.

Of course, he also happens to be an actor, so what he *seems* to be isn't all that reliable.

"Why can't you work Saturday?" I ask, my eyes narrowing.

"You won't even believe it."

"Try me."

"Lou's taking me to see a Broadway show!" Trisha replies in a bubbly voice. "And it was *his* idea. Isn't that amazing?"

"What show?"

"Huh?"

"What show is he taking you to see?"

"*The Puppeteer.*"

If I've caught Trisha in a lie, I have no freaking clue. My ignorance about Broadway musicals, not to mention most pop culture, is definitely the proverbial thorn in my side. I'll have to look it up later. But I find it hard to believe that Trisha would magically want to cover my shift two minutes after Ben announces his plan to take me on a trip.

"So will you do it, Mags?"

"Uh..."

"Please say yes," she begs. "You *know* how much I complain about Lou never paying attention to me. Please let me have this."

A sigh lodges in the back of my throat. Damn it. The guilt card works every time.

"Sure, of course I'll take your shift."

"Great! I owe you a million!"

You bet your ass you do. I hang up the phone and turn my attention back to Ben. "So," I say slowly. "Apparently I now have the day off tomorrow."

His features reveal nothing. "Huh. Looks like fate decided to step in."

"Fate," I repeat, unable to stop the mistrustful cloud swirling in my brain.

He beams at me. "So does this mean the trip is on?"

I take great pleasure in bursting his hope balloon. "Nope."

Pop. The balloon dissolves into an annoyed glimmer. "Why the hell not?"

"I volunteer five days a week. It's a requirement for school, remember?" I shrug. "Fridays and Saturdays are two of those days."

His broad shoulders sag with disappointment. He looks really cute when he's dejected, but I refuse to let that puppy-dog gaze get to me. In fact, this is a conversation I've had so many times, it's almost soothing. The men in my life make demands, my schedule gets in the way, and they leave in a huff. It's a routine now, and the one thing I always gain the most comfort from is my routine.

I soften my tone. "You could still take that trip to...wherever it is you wanted us to go."

"I guess you'll never know," he mutters. For the first time since I've met him, he's lost his confident aura.

The weird pang of guilt in my gut is unwelcome, so I try to ignore it by checking my voicemail. The first one is from a telemarketer, but the second message was left by my supervisor at the Broger Center.

"Maggie, it's Gloria. I really hope you get this message before you show up for your shift tomorrow."

An uneasy feeling climbs up my throat.

"Libby Martin, you know, the little girl with the freckles? Well, she's come down with the chicken pox. I know you haven't had any contact with her lately, but some of the other kids have and they're showing symptoms too. So if you've never had the chicken pox, I'd advise that you don't come in tomorrow."

Fuck you, Fate.

"Actually, don't come for at least a week, just to be safe. The infectious period is about five days, but chicken pox could be dangerous for adults. So stay away if you've never had it, kiddo. Call me to let me know."

I listen to the soft click, and then the automated voice announces I have no other messages.

"Everything okay?" Ben asks warily. He must have noticed my bleak expression.

"Chicken pox," I mumble.

"What?"

"There's a chicken pox outbreak at the center. My boss said if I never had it as a kid, I shouldn't report to work for a week or so."

"Ah. I see." His lips begin to twitch. "So...just out of curiosity...have you ever had the chicken pox?"

I make an inaudible noise, then set my jaw so tight my teeth hurt.

"What was that?" he drawls. "I couldn't make out your answer."

I meet his gaze and see the amusement dancing in his striking blue eyes. "No, Ben, I've never had the chicken pox."

"What a shame." His grin breaks free. "So how long will it take you to pack?"

19

MAGGIE

"Where exactly are we going?" I grumble an hour later. Ben and I are in the back of a cab headed for the airport.

"It's a surprise," he says mysteriously.

"Did I mention I don't like surprises?"

"No, and mentioning it now won't get you any answers." He reaches over and squeezes my lower thigh, and I try to ignore the jolt of desire between my legs. "Trust me, you'll like it. I pulled so many strings I could put the New York Philharmonic out of business."

"That's on you, bud. I never asked to be kidnapped."

Ben rolls his eyes. "Shut it, Red. You agreed to come, fair and square."

He's right. And to be honest, I'm still confused about why I hadn't put up more of a fight. I'm sure I could've come up with more excuses for why I shouldn't leave town, but after my schedule freed up so suddenly, I caved to Ben's pleas and packed a stupid overnight bag.

After the driver drops us off at the International terminal at

La Guardia, Ben takes my bag despite my protests, slinging it over his shoulder. "Ready?"

"How can I be ready when I don't know what to be ready for?"

He grins and pulls the brim of his Yankees cap low to his forehead. I don't blame him for snapping into incognito mode. Hell, I encourage it. We're surrounded by people, and I'm not keen on the idea of him being recognized while I'm at his side

We're met at the end of the taxi stand by a random blonde whose job title—and employer—I'm unsure of. Does she work for Ben? She introduces herself as Sarah and ushers us onto a small private shuttle. As we drive away from the terminal, I shoot Ben a puzzled look.

"Seriously, where are we going?" I insist.

"Be patient, Red."

I make an irritated sound, but force myself to stop asking questions. Arguing with Ben Barrett is about as effective as arguing with a pony.

A few minutes later, we pull up in front of a large private hangar, its doors gaping open to reveal a sleek white airplane.

My jaw drops. "Please don't tell me this is yours," I accuse.

"I'm not that rich," he replies in a mild tone. "But it's a beauty, eh? The Gulfstream IV—sexiest jet ever built, in my opinion. A friend's letting me borrow it."

Borrow it? He talks about *borrowing* a *jet* as if it's a Honda or a fucking Toyota. As we hop out of the shuttle, I can't take my eyes off the plane. Whether or not Ben owns it suddenly becomes a moot point. That he knows someone who does is enough to leave me wide-eyed and speechless.

People actually live like this? I've always known it, but seeing it is an entirely different matter altogether. Seeing it brings a tiny spark of resentment to my gut. I have nothing against someone who can afford a private jet, but it's just a reminder of everything I don't have. I don't aspire to be a jet-setting billionaire who goes through hundred dollar bills like mints, but it would be nice not to worry about saving every penny to pay for basic essentials. The person who owns this plane probably only worries about when it'll be time to trade in for a newer model.

Ben exchanges a few words with the pilot, who greets us at the bottom of the steps by the jet's door. Meanwhile, I sweep my gaze along the length of the aircraft. In gold lettering, scrawled across the side, are the words "PAPA G."

Jeez, does this monstrosity belong to a mobster?

I seriously hope not.

"We're good to go," Ben tells me, shifting my overnight bag to his left shoulder so he can put his arm around me again.

I manage a nod and follow him up the steps leading into the cabin. Inside, I openly gawk at our surroundings. There are about twelve seats in the cabin. White leather, with gold seatbelts that—wait, those can't be real diamonds studded along the buckles, right? Each pair of seats face another, and bolted onto the floor between them are honest-to-God poker tables. With green felt and everything.

"Who owns this?" I blurt out.

"Papa G."

"Who?"

"Papa G." Ben furrows his brows. "You know, the rapper?"

My expression remains blank, causing him to sigh.

"You honestly don't know who Papa G is? LA gangsta rap? 'Where's my Bling, Bitch?'"

I've entered the Twilight Zone. Only thing missing is the creepy music and a guy named Mulder...or is that a different show?

"You're borrowing this plane from a rapper who sings about bitches?" I grumble.

"He doesn't sing, he raps. And yes, I'm borrowing his jet. Papa made a cameo in one of my films last year, so I called in a favor."

"Oh." There is really nothing more to say.

"The flight plan has been filed, and we're all fueled up," the stone-faced pilot says in a professional voice. "If you could take your seats and strap in, we'll be ready for takeoff." He disappears into the cockpit and closes the door.

Ben gestures to one of the window seats. "It's all yours."

I gulp. "No, it's okay, you take it."

"You sure?"

"Uh-huh."

During my gawking of G Pappy's plane, I forgot one very important, very anxiety-inducing thing: I've never flown before.

My knees knock together as I sink into one of the leather chairs and fumble with the seatbelt. Although the temperature in the cabin is cool, my nerves scamper around like an anxious kitten.

I try to assume a calm expression, and then turn to Ben and ask, "How familiar are you with current plane crash statistics?"

"Huh?"

"Plane crashes." I gulp a few times, trying to bring some saliva back into my arid mouth. "How often do they occur? Are smaller planes more likely to go down than larger ones?"

Ben's movie-star mouth stretches in an amazed smile. "Oh man. You're scared of flying?"

"What? No. I mean, I don't know. I've never flown before, so I'm not sure if I'm scared of flying."

A deep laugh rumbles out of his chest. "It'll be fine, babe. You're more likely to get hit by a bus than die in a plane crash. That's a fact."

His reply mollifies me only slightly. My nerves continue gnawing at my stomach, especially when the jet lurches forward and starts wheeling out of the hangar. It rolls toward one of the runways and a second later the pilot's voice crackles over the loudspeaker to announce we're taking off.

I keep my gaze on my lap as the plane speeds down the long strip. When the wheels lift off the runway, my stomach turns. *You have a better chance of getting hit by a bus*, I tell myself, and then repeat the mantra in my head as the jet makes its ascent.

"Just take a quick peek," Ben urges. He places a hand on my chin in an attempt to direct my gaze to the window. "Look how gorgeous the city looks from the air."

Curiosity gets the best of me. I lean across his broad chest and press my nose to the window. "Wow, you're right."

The plane continues to climb into the sky, providing a beautiful view of the cityscape below. Though the sun hasn't quite set entirely, the lights of Manhattan sparkle up at us, the high-rises and skyscrapers growing smaller and smaller the higher we go. The cars speeding across the George Washington Bridge look like the miniature toy cars one of my foster brothers used to play with. Everything looks pretty and surreal, and for the first time all day, a genuine smile reaches my lips.

The smile fades, however, when I realize I'm draped across Ben's chest. That my breasts are squashed into one of his muscular arms. Awareness prickles my skin, searing through my sweater and making my nipples pebble against my thin bra. I know he feels those tight buds, because he slowly moves his arm so that the sleeve of his leather jacket rubs against me.

What is the matter with me? How is it possible that I still haven't gotten enough of this man? He's been staying at my apartment for five days, for Pete's sake. We've already had sex more times than I can count. So how come every time I look at him, every time he looks at me, the desire is as fierce and potent as it was that first night at the hotel?

"It's a great view, isn't it?" he drawls.

I turn to see his blue eyes glued to my mouth. I almost lick my lips in anticipation of his kiss. It embarrasses me how badly I want this man. I should be angry with him for whisking me away when I still have so much work to do, and instead all I can think about is ripping his clothes off.

"Crimson."

I shoot him a look. "What?"

"Crimson," he repeats. "The color of your cheeks. That's the shade of red you turn when you're embarrassed."

"You know how I'm feeling from my cheeks?"

"Yep." He shrugs. "A big part of acting is reading other people's expressions. That way you know how to react."

A *ding* rings through the jet, indicating we can unbuckle our seatbelts.

I cross my legs and give him a thoughtful look. "I keep forgetting you're an actor and not just a celebrity, like the celebrities who aren't famous for anything at all. Though you do fill the celebrity arrogance criteria to a T."

"It's part of my natural charm."

"Keep telling yourself that."

"You know," he says, his features growing serious, "it's really easy to fall into the Hollywood trap once you become famous. You could be the most down-to-earth, kind-hearted person and then you get to Hollywood and your ego inflates like a balloon. Suddenly you're stepping over people to get ahead or drowning in a lifestyle that has the power to kill you. Sex, power, drugs, that sort of thing."

"So how'd you escape the trap?"

"I have a very good mother." He shifts over so we're face to face, and something really wholesome and genuine flickers in his gorgeous eyes. "She always made sure I had a good head on my shoulders, even if it meant slapping it into place."

Envy grips at me, but I try to look unaffected. It isn't Ben's fault I didn't luck out in the maternal role model department, or that my voice will never contain that tinge of love and admiration when I speak of my own mother.

"What about your father?" I ask curiously.

"He ran off with another woman when I was two. Haven't seen him since."

I offer a bitter smile. "Join the club."

"Your dad took off too?"

"My dad wasn't in the picture to begin with. My mother was the one who did the running." I swallow. "I grew up in foster care."

"Did you always live in New York?"

"Yep. Did you always live in Hollywood?"

"Fuck, no. Do you think I'd be this normal if I had? I grew up in Cobb Valley, Ohio, a town with a population of, oh, about two thousand."

"Seriously?"

"Seriously. Most of my classes in high school had about ten kids total." He laughs. "And down the street from my house, there was a drugstore with an honest-to-God malt shop in the back. I'm not making this up."

Hearing Ben talk about his hometown warms my heart. It amazes me that he can talk so unpretentiously about his roots. But I'm also feeling some discomfort now, because being attracted to him is one thing, but getting to know him? Learning about his childhood and chuckling about the malt shop down the street? Telling him about my dismal upbringing? It's too...intimate.

"Can I get you anything to drink?"

I nearly fall out of my seat at the sound of the sugar-sweet female voice. I wasn't aware there was anybody else on board aside from the pilot, and the sudden appearance of a petite blonde in a stewardess uniform makes me wonder who else is hiding in the back of the jet. G Pimp himself?

"I'll take some coffee, please." Ben glances over at me. "Do you want anything, babe?"

I blush. Does the flight attendant know who Ben is? Probably. And he just *babe'd* me, right there in front of the woman.

Ugh. She probably thinks I'm his latest piece of arm candy.

"I want...to use the bathroom," I blurt out, knowing my cheeks have turned crimson all over again.

This entire situation is too surreal for me. The private jet, the movie star, the fact that I'm really starting to *like* the movie star.

Again, way too intimate.

I scurry out of my seat and give the stewardess a fake smile before hurrying toward the lavatory sign at the end of the aisle.

Inside the surprisingly roomy bathroom, I flop down on the closed toilet seat—also a gaudy gold color—and rake both hands through my hair. God, this is so unlike me. How could I have just shoved all my responsibilities aside and agreed to this silly trip? Yeah, I have the day off from work tomorrow and a week-long chicken-pox-induced vacation from the youth center, but think of all the homework I could get out of the way.

Instead, I allowed Ben to whisk me away to...to where? I still have no clue where we're going, and that only bothers me more. I'm not cut out for life without plans and schedules, for spur-of-the-moment decisions and Hollywood actors who make my heart race.

I've seen all those pictures on the web. Ben with a Brazilian supermodel. Ben with a gorgeous soap star. Ben at the Golden Globes. Ben doing the late-night talk-show circuit.

The man is a star. A hot, womanizing star. He has the looks

and the money to make anyone with a pulse drool at his feet, so why is he hanging around with a waitress from Manhattan?

It can't be the thrill of the chase, because truth be told, he's already caught me. He's already broken down my defenses by luring me on this mysterious vacation.

What more can he possibly want?

Before I can attempt to come up with an answer, the door handle clicks and Ben strolls in, oblivious to the stunned look on my face.

I stumble to my feet. "What are you *doing*? What if I was peeing?"

"You weren't," he replies with a shrug. "And if you were, you should've locked the door."

"Because I assumed that all normal, polite people understand that a closed door means *knock*. What are you doing in here?"

"You were taking too long. I was worried you were scheming to find a way to ditch me when we land."

"I wasn't scheming. I was musing."

"About me?"

"No." The lie fills the lavatory, but before Ben can call me on it, I curl my fingers over my hips and don my best I-mean-business expression. "We need to get a few things straight."

"Oh, do we?"

He steps closer, and suddenly the bathroom isn't as roomy as I thought. It's tiny. Oppressive. So tiny and oppressive that Ben's big sexy body is about two inches away from mine, and his stubble-covered chin hovers over my forehead, his warm breath heating the top of my head. And any second now, the growing tent in his jeans is going to poke me in the belly.

It's too tempting, being in an enclosed space with this man.

Being anywhere near him, for that matter.

"We need to set boundaries," I manage to say despite my desert-dry throat.

He licks his bottom lip. "I don't like boundaries, Red."

"I'm sure you don't, but we still need some. I need to know you'll keep your end of the bargain."

"I don't remember any bargains being made." His voice grows rough as he eliminates another inch between us. Now his erection presses against my navel, empirically proving that belly buttons can indeed get turned on.

"I promised you a place to stay. For eight days," I say firmly. "I want you to promise that when the time is up, you'll..."

"I'll what? Leave?"

"Y-yes."

He snakes one hand up my spine, cradles my head, and tilts it so we're eye to eye. With his other hand, he wedges me flush against the wall, and then shoves one denim-clad leg between my thighs.

There's something seriously kinky about the way he's efficiently trapped me in place. He can have his way with me right this second, screw me standing up in the bathroom of a rapper's private jet. The naughty scenario causes a drop of moisture to pool inside my panties, and I know Ben can feel the heat emanating from my core.

"You're ruining the mood," he murmurs, tightening his grip on my waist.

"How am I doing that?"

"You're talking about us parting ways."

"Just promise me we'll say goodbye when the eight days are up." I force out the words, if only to appease my own peace of mind.

"I'll promise later." He wiggles his leg and the friction it creates over my yoga pants drives me mad.

"C'mon, just promise. I told you, I don't want any

complications in my life. You're the boy toy, remember?" It's getting harder to formulate thoughts when he keeps rubbing his thigh against me like that.

"Fine." He slants his head and offers a placating smile. "I promise not to complicate your life."

It isn't the guarantee I asked for, but with my clit swollen from his muscular thigh rubbing against it and my nipples so hard they actually hurt, suddenly the last thing I want to do is talk.

"Ever done it on an airplane?" His voice is silky as a caress, and thick with sexual promise.

"You know the answer to that." I gasp as he tugs at the waistband of my pants and slides them down, along with my underwear, leaving me exposed from below the waist.

"Well, I think we should rectify that."

I wait for him to unzip and thrust inside me, but he doesn't. Instead, he stretches one arm in the direction of the pristine white sink and slides open the drawer beneath it. A second later he holds up a handful of brightly colored condom packets.

"Choose your poison," he teases.

I cup him over the denim and give his hard dick a squeeze. "I choose this one."

He chokes out a groan and shoots me a look so full of hunger I almost come on the spot. Those metallic blue eyes sweep from my flushed face to my slick core, devouring my body in a way that has my knees thumping together.

With an impatient growl, I snatch one of the condoms from his hand, tear open the package and reach for his zipper. He laughs huskily, but I don't care. I can't take it anymore. I'm turned on beyond belief.

I free him from his jeans and roll the latex onto the long length of his cock. "I need you inside me," I order. "Now."

"Yes, ma'am."

He plants one hand on my ass and angles my body for better access. Before I can blink, he slides into my pussy with a thrust so hard and deep that the plane actually shakes. Pleasure rockets through me, and—

Wait a second. The plane is *shaking*?

A light knock raps against the lavatory door. "Mr. Barrett?" comes the flight attendant's voice.

Ben lets out a string of curses so utterly indecent my cheeks grow warm. "You've got to be kidding me," he mutters. He's buried deep inside me, and my inner muscles involuntarily tighten around his cock, causing him to swear again.

He grips my waist to keep me from moving.

"Sorry," I whisper.

"What is it?" he calls at the closed door.

"I'm sorry to disturb you, but the captain just announced we're experiencing some turbulence. It's very light, but you and your guest will need to return to your seats."

Panic jolts through me. Swear to God, if this plane crashes, I'm going to kick Ben Barrett's stupid ass.

Ben mumbles something under his breath.

"What'd you say?" I demand.

"I said fuck."

"Oh."

His lips curve with amusement. "You've really got to stop answering everything with 'oh.'"

"Why the hell are you smiling? Didn't you hear her? We're turbulent!"

He snickers softly. "No, we're experiencing light turbulence." He rocks his hips, and I suddenly remember he's still lodged inside me. "I can be fast. How 'bout you?"

But all my arousal has dissipated. "Are you *insane*?" I hiss, and I'm already wiggling away and bending down to collect my pants. From the corner of my eye, I see Ben's huge cock springing up toward his abs. He's still rock-hard.

"Aw, come on, babe. It's just a bit of turbulence," he complains.

I hurriedly slip into my clothes. "The flight attendant said to return to our seats. I'm not disobeying an order!"

Ben's laughter heats the back of my neck as he eases in behind me. "You are fucking crazy—anyone ever told you that?"

"Why? Because I follow the rules?"

His warm lips plant a kiss on my nape. "Rules are meant to be broken."

I turn around and swat him away. "Put your dick away, Barrett. There's a seatbelt out there with my name on it."

Once he's decent, I open the door to find the flight attendant lurking there, and I'm sure my cheeks are crimson as fuck. As we nonchalantly stroll past the expressionless woman, I try very, very hard to act as if having sex in a private jet lavatory is the most natural thing in the world.

20

BEN

"*I* can't believe we're in the Bahamas," Maggie breathes as we exit the airport terminal a couple of hours later.

I'm struggling to keep up with her energized strides. I practically chase her across Lynden Pindling International Airport, a difficult task considering my balls are still throbbing from being cock-blocked earlier. By fucking *turbulence*, of all things.

We step outside, and a humid breeze instantly rolls over me and pastes my T-shirt to my chest. I hope the hotel manager remembered my request for a change of clothes, otherwise I'm going to be a hot, sweaty mess for the next couple of days.

"Tony's told me so much about the Bahamas, but I never thought I'd get to see it for myself," Maggie remarks.

A muscle twitches in my jaw. "New rule—you're not allowed to mention Two-Time Tony while you're with me."

She cocks her head, causing strands of hair to fall onto her forehead. "Two-Time?"

I brush the red strands away and tuck them behind her ear. "You know, because he only comes two times a year. Literally."

To my surprise, Maggie lets out a loud laugh. Well. Maybe I

should've whisked her away from the city sooner. The island air is already lightening her up.

"So what now?" She stares at the crowd of travelers bustling around and the drivers loading suitcases into the trunks of their cars.

"Now we get into that car right over there"—I point to a black Lincoln—" and we start our trip."

Maggie grins. "Sounds like a plan."

A minute later, we're in the back of the Lincoln and speeding into Nassau toward the marina, where a boat will be waiting for us. The sun begins to set just as we reach the marina, dipping toward the horizon and filling the sky with shades of pink and orange. I hide a smile as an awestruck Maggie stares at the gorgeous sunset. When was the last time she watched the sunset? Knowing her schedule, probably never.

"That's our boat," I say as we get out of the car. I nod to the sleek speedboat docked at the end of the pier.

Maggie visibly gulps. "How familiar are you with current shipwreck statistics?"

I snort. "For fuck's sake, you've never been on a boat either?"

"No," she sighs.

Grinning, I take her hand and lead her down the sturdy wooden planks beneath our feet toward the boat. She seems uneasy as she climbs in, but her expression brightens the moment the driver gives it some gas. The speedboat slices through the calm water, which goes from transparent turquoise to navy-blue under the darkening sky.

I sling an arm over Maggie's shoulders and enjoy the salty breeze hitting my face. The last time I was in the Bahamas was a year ago. I came here with Sonja Reyes, a Brazilian model I'd dated briefly, and I'd been itching to come back ever since.

While the islands boast plenty of celebrity-friendly resorts, I prefer Paradise Bay, which isn't as blatantly lavish as some of the other hotels, but that's why I like it. Private bungalows, deserted beaches, and best of all, the hotel is located near a wildlife reserve, making it hard for trespassers, aka the paparazzi, to loiter around.

"Here we are," the driver calls over his shoulder as he slows the boat and steers toward a long dock nearly hidden by thick foliage.

"Pass me your bag," I tell Maggie.

She does, and I hop onto the wooden pier and extend a hand to help her out. A tall man in a burgundy blazer materializes out of nowhere and strides toward us, greeting me with a firm handshake. "Mr. Barrett, it's good to see you again." He drops a polite kiss on Maggie's knuckles. "Ms. Reilly. I'm Marcus Holtridge, manager of Paradise Bay. Please, follow me."

He leads us to a golf cart, sandwiches himself between us, and signals the driver to go.

The little car maneuvers the lush grounds of the resort, and I feel a rush of satisfaction at the wonder dancing in Maggie's green eyes. I understand her reaction. This place really is gorgeous, with its perfectly manicured lawns, the little cobblestone paths weaving through the luxurious setting, bright exotic flowers everywhere you look. When Sonja first brought me here, I thought I'd died and gone to Eden.

We motor past a man-made waterfall that flows into a small pond. Maggie nudges my arm and gestures to the school of fat koi swimming in the water. "Isn't that pretty?" she says happily.

I sweep my gaze over her rosy cheeks. "Sure is."

Marcus points out various points of interest. The tennis courts, the spa, the small but elegant casino where I lost five grand the last time I'd come. This is the perfect place to relax without worrying about your face being splashed on every newspaper in the country. And considering I promised my agent I'd lay low, I couldn't have picked a better atmosphere to do that in.

We finally reach our destination—a pale yellow bungalow nestled between majestic fronds, picturesque and private. The little house stands on a stretch of clean white sand, steps away from the ocean. Last time I was here, I left all the windows open at night, and the sound of the waves lapping against the shore lulled me to sleep.

"This is beautiful," Maggie confesses as we step into the large spacious room. Holtridge and the golf cart have discreetly left us to our own devices.

A billowing white canopy hangs from the ceiling and drapes over the frame of the big mahogany bed. On the blue bedspread sits a wicker basket filled with fragrant soaps, papaya shampoos, face towels and other welcome items.

I drop Maggie's overnight bag on the polished floor. "You should see the hot tub."

"Hot tub?"

"Follow me."

I lead her to the glass doors across the room and point.

"You've got to be kidding me," she says as her gaze follows my outstretched finger. The four-person hot tub, skillfully built under a cluster of palm trees and surrounded by boulders, gives it the appearance of a natural rock pool.

"What do you say we get into our suits and hop in?"

"I didn't bring a swimsuit."

"Don't worry, when I asked the manager to leave a change of clothes for me, I made sure to request a few bikinis too. Go take your pick."

"How'd you pull all this together so quickly?"

I shrug. "I'm Ben Barrett, remember?"

As Maggie drifts over to the tall oak armoire, I walk toward the nightstand and reach for the telephone. "I'm going to make a quick call while you get changed."

I dial my agent's number and wait. From the corner of my eye I see Maggie grab one of the bathing suits off a hanger and—is she actually going into the bathroom to change? Christ. Like I haven't already seen her naked a dozen times.

"Fuck, Ben, where are you now?" Stu demands without saying hello.

"The Bahamas," I reply.

"Wonderful. Absolutely frickin' wonderful for you. It warms my heart that you're sunbathing on a beach while I'm working my ass off here."

"I thought you convinced the media I wasn't abducted."

"I did, but they still think you're up to something fishy. The prostitute angle is old news. So is the elopement with the mysterious hotel chick. Now the consensus is that you're shacked up with another married broad."

"I was never shacked up with a married broad before."

"Of course not."

My jaw tightens. Stu has been my agent for nine years and counting, and the man seriously doesn't have faith in me?

"There have been a few positive developments, though," Stu says, his tone all business now.

"Yeah, like what?"

"Two high-budget screenplays landed on my desk, and the studio contacted me about a sequel for *McLeod's Revenge*."

"Are you joking? *McLeod's Revenge Two*? The guy already got his damn revenge, what more is he after?"

"Who cares? It's money in our pockets."

Is it possible to loathe one little phrase this badly? I'm so sick of talking about money. What happened to artistic expression? Thought-provoking, quality scripts? Challenging roles?

"Oh, and Alan Goodrich wants to meet with you."

I almost drop the phone. "What?"

"He called to set up an appointment."

"Business or personal?"

"He didn't say. But, seeing as you were screwing his wife, I doubt he wants to meet up so he can offer you a part in his new World War Two epic."

"Goodbye, Stu."

I hang up the phone before I say something I'll regret. My insides churn with the slow boil of injustice I've swallowed back for months now. If I wanted to, I could phone up all the major media outlets and set the record straight about Gretchen, the inheritance and the reasons behind the whole goddamn mess.

But I don't want to.

Let the world think what they want of me. Let them say whatever they feel like saying about me. My private matters aren't anybody's business but my own.

"You okay?"

Maggie's soft voice brings me back to the present. She stands at the bathroom door, a towel wrapped around her waist and tucked under her breasts.

"I'm fine. Just checking in with my agent."

"Did I hear you talking about a movie sequel? That sounds cool."

I stride toward the armoire and rummage around until I find a pair of swim trunks. The staff has also supplied me with a stack of clean clothing. Jeans, T-shirts, boxers, even a crisp black tuxedo draped on one of the hangers. The tux gives me an idea, which I store in the back of my brain as I quickly peel off my shirt.

"I guess it would be cool," I respond, "if I wasn't turning down the part."

"Why would you turn down—" Her voice halts the second I drop my pants.

"Everything okay?" Chuckling at the tantalizing blush on her cheeks, I slowly slip into my swim trunks, tugging at the material when it snags over my growing erection.

"You have no shame," she grumbles, openly staring at my cock.

"Nope." I tighten the drawstring and step toward her. "Now can we please get in that hot tub and finish what we started on the jet?"

21

MAGGIE

I have never been so excited to be naked before. Well, not fully naked. I'm wearing this indecent string bikini as I lower my body into the bubbling water, and Ben has his trunks on as he joins me. But we don't need to be naked for me to know we're about to have wild, sweaty, hot tub sex. I honestly can't wait. Since I met Ben, I've had sex in more new places than I can count: the shower, the kitchen counter, the living room floor, a private jet. Might as well add hot tub to the growing list.

"I want to tear that bikini off with my teeth."

"What?" I shiver despite the near-boiling water lapping against my body.

Ben shoots me an endearing smile. "Did I say that out loud?"

"Yup."

"Can't fault a guy for being honest."

I shift so that one of the jets presses directly against my tailbone, and my muscles turn to jelly as the pressure slowly massages my skin. Overhead, a spatter of bright stars lights up the clear night sky. I tilt my head to take in the gorgeous view, breathing in the scent of salt and earth.

This is nice. I hadn't wanted it to be nice, but it is. I haven't taken a vacation in...well, I've *never* taken a vacation. The strange rush of relaxation coursing through me feels completely foreign.

"You're too far away," Ben complains.

With a roll of my eyes, I scoot over so we're side by side. Arm touching arm. Thigh against thigh.

He instantly drapes one wet arm around my bare shoulders and slides his hand to give one of my boobs a firm squeeze. "Much better." He slants his head and shoots me a mischievous look. "Wanna make out?"

I laugh. "Sure. Maybe afterwards we could go to the malt shop and share a milkshake with two straws."

He doesn't seem to mind my teasing. If anything, his grin only widens and, as usual, he wastes no time covering my mouth with his.

I'm not sure I'll ever get used to this man's kisses. They're long and intoxicating. Hurried. Rough. Taking it slow? I doubt he knows what that means. Oh no. His lips and tongue simply take what they want without permission.

Not that I mind. His hungry claim of my mouth steals the breath from my lungs and makes my chest constrict with burning need. Each hot, toe-curling kiss ends with a gasp from me and a groan from him, until I'm squirming in the warm water eddying around me.

Pulling back, Ben nips playfully at my earlobe. "Why do you still have that bikini on?"

"I'm waiting for you to tear it off with your teeth, remember?"

"Is that a challenge?"

"More like a dare."

"I like the way you think, Red."

Water splashes over the edge of the hot tub as Ben moves in front of me. He rests on his knees, his chiseled torso disappearing into the water with a splash of clear bubbles. "I'll begin with your bottoms," he says, his voice professional and matter-of-fact.

The last thing I see before he ducks under the water is the dirty grin on his face. I jump when his mouth latches onto my hip and tugs at the strings holding my bottoms together. His teeth graze my skin. He tugs again and then one half of the triangle comes loose.

Ben surfaces, wiping droplets off his handsome face. His expression is weirdly grim. "I'm sorry to inform you that I couldn't save the knot to the right of your hip, Ms. Reilly. I have high hopes for the left one, however."

I choke back a laugh as he submerges again, and then shiver when he unties the other side. The bikini bottoms float to the surface at the same time as my mischievous movie star.

"Couldn't save the left one either. It's gone," he says, pointing to the shiny green material as a current of water carries it away to the other side of the rock pool.

"You're a sad excuse for a doctor," I say with mock anger.

"That's what the producers at *General Hospital* said before they fired me," he answers with a rueful smile. "I couldn't pronounce *chronic inflammatory demyelinating polyneuropathy*."

"What on earth is that?"

"To this day I still don't know. But I sure as fuck know how to say it now." He winks and then lowers his gaze to my boobs, which are still covered. "I should take care of that."

He skims his fingers over my wet shoulders and maneuvers me so that my back is to him. I close my eyes and inhale deeply, waiting for the sting of his teeth against my skin. A shaky breath slips free when my top comes loose and my breasts are bared.

My nipples instantly jut out, hardening even more when I shift and one of the jets blasts a gushing rush of heat right against my chest.

"So...your bikini is dunzo," Ben whispers into my neck. "What should I bite next?"

I twist around to look at him. "Are you going to do that all night?"

"Do what?"

"Narrate."

"Why, does it turn you on?"

I mull it over. "I'm actually pretty indifferent to it."

"Indifferent? No woman of mine is ever allowed to feel indifference in my presence, babe."

No woman of mine?

Before I can figure that one out, Ben brushes a light kiss over my lips. "Trust me, babe, by the time I'm finished with you, you're going to love my narration." Then he reaches down and cups my breasts. "Now hush. Your tits require my attention."

A jolt of desire streaks across my belly and settles into an impatient throb between my legs.

With a roguish smile, he dips lower into the water and sucks one of my nipples between his lips. A breath blows out of my mouth and dissolves into the steam rising from the hot tub. Ben's tongue begins a torturous assault on my nipples, licking and swirling, sucking and nipping. Each time the scrape of his teeth brings a delicious sting of pain, he licks and kisses it away, driving me crazy with need, until I give a primitive cry and sink under the water like a lump of clay.

With a chuckle, he grabs my hips and raises me up. "I think it's time for my fingers to get involved," he says with a decisive nod.

The bubbles from the jets restrict me from seeing his hand, but I sure as hell feel it. Feel his fingers running down my slit, feel his thumb rubbing circles over my clit.

The throbbing grows worse. "No fingers," I choke out. "I need more."

"Sorry, we haven't reached that part of the narrative yet." He offers an apologetic shrug and continues his exploration of my pussy.

I groan and fumble for the waistband of his trunks. "I hate you."

"No, you don't." He skillfully pushes my roaming hand away. "And stop interfering."

I almost bristle at his commanding tone, but the hunger swarming his gaze stops me. It's obvious he wants me, and for a girl who's never been wanted all her life, I experience a sense of pride from his lust-filled expression.

I grip his broad shoulders and rock my hips to meet the wicked thrusts of his fingers. I'm all but riding his hand, and the orgasm hits me hard and fast, a wave of pleasure rippling through my body as I clamp my lips together to stop from crying out. I gasp for air, inhaling a cloud of steam that warms my cheeks. Heat consumes my body, heat from the fire of pleasure between my legs, from the water surrounding my body, and the island breeze kissing my face.

"So, I think—" Ben starts.

"No more talking," I order, rising from the tub on unsteady feet.

"Where are you going?"

"Inside. Where I'm going to lie naked on the bed. And you're going to follow me, and take those damn trunks off, and then we're going to fuck each other's brains out." I roll my eyes. "How's that for a narrative?"

Ben grins. Without another word, he pinches my bare ass

and chases me into the bungalow. As I promised, I stretch out on the bed, naked and wet, watching as he reaches for the waistband of his swim trunks. A second later, he's gloriously naked, all tanned skin and hard muscle and tattoos. And his dick is so hard, my inner muscles give an involuntary clench.

The teasing light leaves his blue eyes, replaced with another dose of pure, unrestrained hunger. I shiver under his hot stare, feeling like Little Red Riding Hood about to be consumed whole by the big bad wolf.

He sheathes himself with a condom that seems to materialize out of nowhere. Then he lowers himself on top of me and rubs the tip of his cock over my swollen pussy.

"Maggie," he rasps.

I wait for him to say something more, but he doesn't. Instead, he tangles one hand in my damp hair, places the other on my hip, and kisses me at the same time he drives deep inside me.

My body stretches to accommodate him, and I instantly squeeze my muscles around his shaft and arch my hips to bring him deeper. He groans and digs his fingers into my waist, then slides all the way out only to pump right back in with a greedy thrust. My gaze strays to his biceps, where his tats seem to vibrate each time he flexes.

His eyes narrow into slits. "Fuck," he croaks. And then he stops moving.

I grin up at him. "You're close?"

He responds with a mumbled expletive.

I slide my hands down his sinewy back. He's got muscles in places I didn't even know had muscles. "What are you waiting for then?"

"You."

"Me what?"

"I'm waiting for you to tell me just how much you want it."

He rotates his hips and then withdraws again, his pace excruciatingly slow.

A shockwave rocks my core, causing me to squeeze his tight ass and buck against him. Suddenly I don't have the energy to tease or prolong the inevitable.

"I want it very, very badly," I whisper.

With a satisfied nod, he plunges into me and swallows my strangled cry with a hard kiss. His mouth devours mine, his fingers stroking my hair and my hips and my clit. I drink in his kisses and it isn't long before waves of pleasure crash over me again. A climax so extraordinary that my legs shake and bright light explodes in front of my eyes.

The bliss only deepens when I feel Ben shudder, when I hear the low groan signaling that he's coming. I tighten my grip around his neck. When I press my breasts to his sweat-soaked chest, the erratic thumping of his heartbeat vibrates against my skin.

I don't know how long we lie there, and I don't care that the crush of his powerful chest restricts the flow of oxygen to my brain. I like the weight of him. And the slick feel of him. And the spicy masculine scent of him. I know I should move, get up, get dressed, put an end to this intimate moment, but I can't bring myself to do it. Instead, I release a sigh and stroke his back, pressing my face to his chest as he slowly rolls over and brings me with him.

22

BEN

I'm reeling, not so much from the incredible sex, but from Maggie's odd behavior. Something's changed. I can't put my finger on it, but I sense it as I hold Maggie in my arms and thread my fingers through her hair. Somehow, in the minutes we've been lying here recovering from our mind-blowing orgasms, she's dropped her guard. She didn't jump out of the bed after the sex, didn't start rambling on about her schedule and schoolwork and all the reasons why being here with me is a bad idea.

She just curled up beside me, letting me stroke her hair.

I like it.

A lot.

"So what now?" she asks after giving a big yawn. "Should we take a walk on the beach?"

"Says the redhead after yawning her face off," I tease. "It's okay to be tired, babe. To just lie around and do nothing."

She shifts, moving onto her side so that her gaze locks with mine. Her expression reflects uneasiness. "Doing nothing makes me anxious."

I grin. "I've noticed."

"It's not a bad thing, is it?"

"No, it's not a bad thing. No need to get defensive." I reach for her leg and lift it so that it's draped over my thighs, not sure why I need the physical contact so desperately. "I just think you need to learn how to relax every now and then."

She doesn't answer, but the troubled look on her face speaks volumes. I wonder how many times she's heard that before from the people in her life. Her friends. Co-workers. That dumbass Tony. I'd bet anything that Maggie's non-existent love life is a direct result of her need to always be doing something.

"What do you want from your life?" I find myself asking. "Aside from being a social worker?"

Surprise flickers in her gaze, followed by a glimmer of confusion. "To be honest, I've never really thought past the career thing."

"You don't think about getting married? Or having children? Traveling, gardening, anything that doesn't involve working?"

"Not really." Before I can question the response, she turns the tables on me. "What about you? Do you ever think of a life beyond acting?"

"All the time." A wry smile creases my mouth. "If I'm being honest, acting is definitely not what I thought it would be."

"What did you hope to get from it?"

I pause to think. Shit. I've never let myself examine the hopes I had going into this industry. Or the unhappiness I feel now that my career has zigzagged in a direction I never wanted.

"Ben?"

I chew on the inside of my cheek, trying to put it into words I've never said out loud. "It's...it's like I bought a first-class ticket for passage on the Titanic," I finally say. "You know, boarding the ship, getting caught up in the splendor of it, thinking I'm on top of the world. And then comes the iceberg and the ship sinks."

"So what's your iceberg?" she asks, reaching out to touch my chin.

I haven't shaved in days, and the feel of Maggie's fingers skimming my rough beard makes my groin tighten. She doesn't miss the way my cock jerks in response, but she wiggles her eyebrows and gives me a no-nonsense stare. "Oh no. We're having a conversation. Stop trying to distract me."

I protest. "I didn't do anything."

"No, but he did." She stares at my cock for a moment, and then shakes her head as if to snap herself out of it. "So...the iceberg?"

"Being typecast," I admit. "I started acting because I loved it, but I also wanted to be recognized. Respected. Then I did one action flick and suddenly I'm known as bad boy macho man Ben Barrett. I haven't been offered a decent role in years. All I get are mindless let's-blow-up-every-possible-thing-we-can films."

She smiles dryly. "Not that I have much experience in the film industry, but one thing I've learned in life is that nobody's going to give it to you. If you want something, you go after it."

"I'm trying," I answer in frustration.

"Try harder."

Amazement washes over me. Maggie isn't like any other chick I've been with. The women I know would either laugh it off and tell me to enjoy the money, or make a heartfelt speech about how one day someone will recognize my talent and give me a significant role. Not Maggie. Nope, she tells me to *try harder*.

Oddly enough, it's just what I want—and need—to hear.

She yawns again. "You're right. I'm tired," she announces. "No beach walking tonight."

We're both still naked, but Maggie doesn't seem to mind. Without an ounce of bashfulness, she stretches one arm toward the end table and fumbles for the remote control.

"Let's watch a movie," she says. "I haven't watched a movie in ages."

Although I'd prefer a repeat performance of what we'd done a half hour ago, I decide to let Maggie enjoy herself. If watching movies will finally make her relax, then why not.

But when she flicks on the TV, the first thing that flashes across the screen is my face.

"Hey, it's one of your movies," she exclaims. Before I can object, she raises the volume and a crack of fake gunfire fills the bungalow. "Oh, wow. You're right about all the explosions."

Seeing my latest film on the screen leaves me weary, but Maggie seems to be enjoying it so I stay quiet. I pull her closer, wrapping one arm around her, and turn my gaze to the movie, inwardly cringing at every loud blast and the screeching tires from the car chase I loathed shooting. I do most of my own stunts, and I went home that night covered in bruises and needing to ice my ribcage.

The film drags on, and next to me Maggie's body grows warmer and her breathing evens out. She's fallen asleep. I try to fight back a prickle of insult, but it's hard. My movies suck so bad they even make Maggie, the workaholic Energizer bunny, fall asleep. That hurts more than I'll ever admit.

Trying not to wake her, I slowly take the remote control next to her sleeping body and turn off the TV. Then I reach for the lamp beside me and turn that off too. Darkness engulfs the room, save for one clear shaft of moonlight that pours in through the sheer curtains.

With a sigh, I close my eyes and stroke Maggie's hair again.

Just as I start to drift off, her soft voice breaks through the silence in the room.

"You're a good actor, Ben," she murmurs, giving me a little squeeze before she falls back asleep.

23

MAGGIE

"I don't think I'll ever get used to this," I declare the next evening.

I collapse on the bed, my stomach full from the eight-course dinner we just indulged in and my skin pink from the hours we spent in the sun today.

"Get used to what?" Ben closes the door and heads for the plush leather armchair near the bed. He drops into it with a contented sigh.

"This." I wave my hand around. "Our own private bungalow. Our own private stretch of sand. Being waited on at dinner. Eating steak and lobster."

Having wild, almost hourly sex with a movie star... I keep that part to myself. His ego is already big enough.

"And to think," he says with a chuckle, "we still have the whole night in front of us. You should hop in the shower, by the way. It's almost time."

My head comes up with a jerk. "Almost time for what?"

"It's a surprise."

"You know I don't like surprises."

"And I don't like tennis, but I played a few sets with you, didn't I?"

The memory brings a smile to my lips. Earlier I told Ben I hadn't played tennis since high school, and although he'd griped and grumbled the entire time, he spent two hours on the court with me. Which was really sweet coming from a man who could barely serve the ball without hitting the net. Still, his pitiful tennis skills—and candid admission of inadequacy— were seriously charming.

I prop myself up on my elbows and sigh. "I'm too full to move. I'll shower later."

"No time. We're on a schedule, Red."

"Oh, are we?" I roll my eyes.

"Yep." He rises from his chair and gives one of my arms a tug, dragging me off the bed. "So get your pretty little ass into that shower."

"You're not going to join me?"

He shakes his head. "There are a few details I need to take care of."

I can't help but pout. "Fine."

I drift into the bathroom and slip out of my yellow sundress. I hang it on the hook behind the door, then step into the black-tiled shower stall next to the marble bathtub. As the warm water sluices over my sun-kissed body, I lather lavender body wash on my skin.

I haven't felt this relaxed in years. Actually, I haven't felt this relaxed ever, seeing as my life is a big ball of stress that revolves around work and school. Relaxation has never been part of the equation.

I have to force myself to remember that although I'm enjoying my time at the resort, my time with Ben, it's not about to become part of my routine. I can't forget where I come from. What I'll be going back to when this trip ends.

My schedule, not to mention my finances, doesn't allow for impromptu island getaways and sweaty sex with celebrities. It's easy to lose myself in these luxurious surroundings, but luxury isn't something I can count on. What happens if I lose my job or fail my exams? Ben has his big pile of money to cushion his fall, but what do I have?

Myself. No family, no roots, no security blankets. I have only myself, and I need to remember that before I get caught up in all this glitz and glamour, or start to believe that a girl like me might actually belong in Ben Barrett's life.

~

"Mimi is here to do your hair and makeup."

I move my gaze from my newly polished fingernails and fight back a yawn. "Is he trying to kill me?"

Denise, the petite blonde who's been shuffling me around the spa for the past couple of hours, gives a rueful smile. "You weren't kidding—you really are one of those women who can't handle being pampered." There's a teasing lilt to her voice.

"Is that what you call being poked and prodded for two hours? Pampered?"

She wags her finger. "Don't pretend you didn't like it. I saw your face during the mud bath. You enjoyed it." She takes a step back. "I'll send Mimi in."

I wait for Denise to leave before releasing a sigh of contentment. Fine, so I enjoyed the mud bath. And the massage from Paulo the heartthrob. Maybe even the manicure and pedicure.

Okay, I enjoyed it all.

When Ben dropped me off at the spa, I'd ordered myself to have a bad time. To hate every second of the experience and laugh in the face of luxury. But I failed. I've wholeheartedly relished every tranquil, self-indulgent moment.

"I'm here to do your hair." A willowy brunette with a stunning olive complexion strides into the room carrying a large silver case.

I narrow my eyes suspiciously. "Why exactly am I getting my hair done?"

Mimi shrugs. "Afraid I don't know. Mr. Barrett never said."

"Of course he didn't."

I settle back in the plush leather chair and decide there's no point questioning Ben's motives. I don't voice one complaint, not even when Mimi nearly scalps me trying to twist my unruly hair into a French twist. And I don't flinch when the woman goes at my eyebrows with a pair of mean-looking tweezers.

An hour later, Mimi finally finishes styling my hair and applying my makeup. But just when I get to my feet thinking we're done, she holds up her hand.

"One more thing."

I pinch the bridge of my nose, the one part of my face I can touch without ruining my makeup. "I've been in this spa for three hours, what more can he want to do to me?"

Mimi smiles, leaves the room, and quickly returns with a garment bag and a shoebox. "He wants you to get dressed."

I probably would've made another sarcastic comment if it weren't for the spectacular item the hairstylist removes from the bag. I stare at the slinky, emerald green dress. It's *gorgeous*, more gorgeous than anything I own. Or have ever owned.

"Versace," Mimi supplies, seeing the wonder in my eyes. She drapes the dress over the back of the chair. "I'll leave you to get dressed."

The second the door closes, I waste no time whipping off my over-sized terrycloth robe. I carefully wiggle into the Versace masterpiece, then spin around to examine my reflection in the full-length mirror.

Wow.

With my hair piled atop my head and the gorgeous satin material clinging to my curves, I look like a different person.

"Oh my, I believe Mimi deserves a raise." Denise's voice comes from the doorway.

I blush as I meet her admiring stare. "You think I look good?"

"I think you look fabulous," she corrects. She gives one last appraising look, and then gestures for me to follow her. "Mr. Barrett asked for you to meet him in the lobby at midnight. You don't want to be late."

I glance down at my bare feet. "But I don't have shoes."

Denise points to the shoebox the hairdresser left behind. "Sure you do."

Feeling like a kid on Christmas morning, I make a beeline for the narrow box. Unlike the hand-me-down gifts I received from my foster families over the years, this box contains something new and shiny. Silver, high-heeled sandals that match the silver eye shadow Mimi dabbed on my eyelids. Ben obviously planned everything to a T.

I slip on the shoes and follow Denise out the door, oddly self-conscious as we leave the spa. My heels click against the marble floor beneath them, and my heartbeat drums in my throat as we near the majestic lobby of the resort.

"I feel like a princess," I whisper, shooting a nervous glance at the woman next to me.

She stops in front of the arch leading into the lobby. "And there's your prince," she whispers back.

I shift my gaze and see him. Leaning casually against one of the stone pillars in the middle of the large room, his hawk-like gaze drilling into me.

My surroundings fade as our eyes lock, and I don't break eye contact as I walk across the room toward Ben.

"You look...fuck, Maggie," he mumbles. "You look beautiful."

Heat spills through me. I have to admit, as out of my depth as I feel in the elegant dress he bought for me, I like the effect it has. The neckline dips so low that my breasts practically spill out of the silk bodice, and the slit up the side shows a hell of a lot of thigh. It's the kind of dress meant to tease a man into submission, and though I'll never be a hundred percent comfortable dressing like a vixen, I like the delight I see in Ben's blue eyes.

I also like the tuxedo currently hugging his lean body, the way the black jacket stretches over his broad shoulders and emphasizes his rock-hard chest. With that classy tux and his clean-shaven face, he looks every inch the movie star he is, and again I feel like Cinderella as I accept his proffered arm and curl my fingers around his biceps.

"Did you have fun at the spa?" he asks as we fall into step together.

"Yes."

"Good."

He leads me across the lobby toward a set of heavy oak doors flanked by two large men in dark suits. At our approach, the men pull the doors open with a graceful swoop and gesture for us to enter. Seeing as how we're dressed like we're going to the prom, I expect to walk into a grand ballroom. To my surprise, it's a casino.

And not the kind of casino you see in Las Vegas, with flashing neon lights and ear-piercing chimes and bells of slot machines. This one is small and sophisticated, with an array of game tables, waiters with trays of champagne, and a black-tie clientele. Aside from the occasional jubilant cry coming from the roulette section, the atmosphere is serious yet relaxed, and it practically oozes money.

"Do you like to gamble?" Ben asks. We cross the plush carpeted floor toward one of the blackjack tables.

"I don't know. I've never gambled before."

What would I have to gamble with? I almost add, but stop myself just in time. A man as wealthy as Ben wouldn't understand anyway.

"Trust me. You'll like it."

We stop in front of a table. A suit-clad man approaches and exchanges a few words with Ben. They speak in murmured tones, but I catch the word "markers" and then raise my brows at the number "two thousand."

As a bow-tied card dealer doles out a stack of chips and places them in front of Ben, I lean over and whisper, "Did you just ask for two thousand dollars' worth of chips?"

"Yep." He splits the stack in half and pushes one pile toward me. "This one's yours."

I gulp. "I can't take your money. What if I lose?"

"Then you lose."

My throat tightens with irritation. "I won't be in debt to you, Ben."

"Call it a gift."

"A thousand-dollar stack of chips is not a gift." Setting my jaw, I push the red circles back toward Ben's pile. "I can't accept it."

He pauses for a moment, and then sighs. "Fine, be difficult. We'll play as a team."

"And I won't keep a dime of the winnings," I say firmly.

"And you won't keep a dime of the winnings," he echoes, albeit grudgingly.

The dealer's lips twitch, and I suspect he finds the entire

exchange amusing. He's probably never encountered a chick so willing to kiss a thousand bucks goodbye.

"Ready to play some cards?" he asks politely, glancing from me to Ben.

We spend the next hour at the blackjack table, with Ben explaining the game to me with the utmost patience. After a few big wins, I start to relax. I smile at the tuxedo-clad men who join us, sip a glass of champagne, and stare at a familiar-looking woman in a gold sequined dress for ten minutes before Ben finally whispers that she's an anchor at CNN.

"You do watch the news, don't you?" he teases.

"Sometimes."

The laugh he gives sends a flurry of shivers up my spine. "Don't you feel alienated sometimes, being so out of touch with the world?"

I shrug. "I'm too busy to feel alienated."

He tweaks one of the wavy tendrils framing my cheeks. "We really need to talk about this jam-packed schedule of yours."

My reply is cut off by the sound of a female voice squealing, *"Benjamin?"*

An unbelievably tall, unbelievably beautiful woman with raven hair and sparkling blue eyes saunters over in an indecent red dress and a pair of six-inch heels. Before I can blink, the giant sexpot throws her arms around Ben and splatters kisses on his cheeks.

"Benjamin! It is you!" With her heavy accent, it sounds more like *"Ben-ja-meeen, eet eeez you!"*

Something about the way her eyes twinkle suggestively hints that this beauty knows Ben on a very intimate level. In fact, after a closer examination of her face, I realize she's the supermodel at Ben's side in the picture I found on the Internet.

"Sonja," Ben says in a warm voice, while gingerly

disentangling himself from her embrace, "I should've known I'd run into you here."

"Well, of course. This is my second home! Do you remember the first time we came here, Benjamin?" Sonja licks her bottom lip, a move so blatantly sexual I want to tear out her tongue.

Meow.

"And who is your lovely friend?" she adds, sparing me a brief look.

I have to hand it to the woman. She makes the phrase "lovely friend" seem like the most contemptible insult ever composed.

"This is Maggie." Ben's features are strained, discomfort evident in his eyes.

"It is wonderful to meet you, Maggie."

Wow, even my name coming out of Sonja's lush red lips sounds like an affront.

"Yeah, same here," I reply.

"And what do you do?" she presses, and there's something a bit catty in her eyes. "Judging by the way you look in that dress, I'm going to guess you're a model?"

I swallow, feeling horribly exposed as Sonja looks me up and down. "Actually, I'm a waitress. From New York."

There's a moment's silence. Then it's broken by a long tinkling laugh from Sonja.

She turns to grin at Ben. "So you're—how do you Americans say it? Slumming it?"

The callous words slice into my chest and cause my breath to jam in my throat. I no longer feel exposed. I feel humiliated, and even though nobody is looking our way, I feel like every eye in the room is glued on me.

My hands tremble slightly. I want to slap this bitch the way I slapped Robbie Hanson when he called me a foster-freak back in the ninth grade, but for the life of me I can't make my vocal cords work. So I do the only other thing I can think of. I mutter, "Will you excuse me, please?"

And then I straighten my shoulders, lift my chin, and walk away as steadily as my legs will allow and with as much dignity as I can muster.

"*O*opsy. I seem to have upset your little friend."

My heart shrinks as I stare after Maggie's retreating back. Next to me, Sonja looks pleased with herself, which makes me rethink every positive thing I've ever thought of the woman. She's a snob, sure. Self-absorbed, totally. But I never took her for downright nasty.

"That was uncalled for," I say coolly.

Sonja just laughs. "Oh, Benjamin, I was only—how do you say?—goofing around. Your friend is much too sensitive. This is why you need a real woman, *caro*."

"I have a real woman." I hook my thumb at the exit. "She went thataway."

Without another word, I leave Sonja at the blackjack table and march out of the casino, quickening my stride when I enter the lobby and find it empty. One of the clerks at the front desk discreetly nods toward the glass doors at the entrance.

I step outside in time to see Maggie stalking toward the golf cart in front of the building. She looks so achingly beautiful in that green dress, so goddamn sexy in those strappy heels, that I have to restrain myself from pulling her into my arms and kissing the fuck out of her.

She isn't crying, but the look of ice she gives me when she notices my presence clearly says, *Back off.*

"Maggie..." I start timidly.

She bunches the hem of the dress with her hands so it doesn't drag on the ground on her way to the waiting cart. "Don't worry. It's not your fault she spoke the truth."

I almost keel over backwards. "What? You think what she said was the truth—"

She flops onto the back of the golf cart and signals the driver.

Chest tight with anger, I push forward and leap into the little car before it speeds off. I force myself to take a calming breath, but it doesn't ease the tension constricting my jaw. "There wasn't an ounce of truth to what Sonja said," I argue, stunned that Maggie would even suggest it.

"Maybe not. But it is something I've been wondering myself." Maggie sounds frustrated. "What are you *doing* with me, Ben? You're a movie star, I'm a waitress. You've got millions of dollars in your bank account, I'm lucky to see a hundred in mine. You know Brazilian supermodels and famous rappers, I spend my days with poor and abused kids." She lets out a strangled sigh and scrunches up the material of her dress with one hand. "This isn't me, Ben. This dress. Being pampered in a spa. Throwing away money at casinos. It's not me, and you don't seem to get that."

"I don't seem to get it?" I'm growing angry again. "Why would I? From the day we met I've been trying to impress you! And since nothing else seemed to work, I thought maybe I'd have some luck with whisking you away to a tropical island." I roll my eyes bitterly. "My bad, apparently."

"Why would you want to impress me?" Her voice comes out strained. "I...I don't get what you want from me."

I can see her pulse thudding in her throat, hear the ragged breaths exiting her mouth, and a thread of confusion stitches my insides. She's just raised the one question I've been avoiding for days.

What do I want from her?

Sex would've been the answer a week ago.

More sex would've been the answer last night.

But, if I'm honest with myself, maybe it's always been about more than sex. I liked Maggie from the first moment I met her. Liked her sass, her confidence, her complete disinterest in my celebrity lifestyle. I like that she isn't scared to tell me off, and I especially like how she makes me work. For her body, her trust, her time. Women constantly throw themselves at my feet, but not Maggie. She knows who she is and what she wants, and she isn't afraid to say it. That's probably what I like most of all.

"I want to spend time with you." I rake my fingers through my hair, frazzled. "I'm with you because I like you. Because you're... real. Don't you get it? I'm surrounded by plastic people. Fake, shallow people who think they know me, who pretend they care about knowing me. Do you realize you're the first person other than a reporter who actually wanted to know where I grew up?"

She doesn't answer.

"Hell, even my own agent doesn't bother to dig deeper." My mouth twists in a frown. "He hasn't once asked for details about Gretchen Goodrich and that money. He just assumes—like the rest of the world—that I fucked her."

"And you expected something different?" Maggie says wearily. "You've got a reputation for sleeping around. It's really not so shocking that people believe you went to bed with a married woman."

Something inside me hardens. "And what about you? Do you believe that line of bull?"

"I don't know what to believe. I don't know you, outside of the biblical sense."

My nostrils flare at her dismissive tone. "You're saying that in the entire week we've spent together, you didn't get a single sense of who I am? That I might be a decent guy?"

She tilts her head and offers a look full of distress and far too much wisdom for her age. "Very few people are decent, Ben. In the end, the only person you can count on is yourself. Sex, relationships, even love, they're not tangible, they disappear in the blink of an eye."

"So, what, you avoid it all for fear that it might disappear?" I shake my head. "Is that why you hide behind your job and your volunteer work and college, because those are the only things you can count on?"

She just frowns.

I inhale the humid night air. "Well, I call bullshit. You *can* count on relationships and other people to be there for you. Some connections can never be broken. Look at my mom, for instance. She had a hard life, raised me on her own, struggled to put food on the table, and she never complained, never packed up and left, even though I know there were times she must have felt like it."

"You want to talk about mothers?" Maggie shoots back. "Well, mine abandoned me in front of a gas station when I was five. She told me to wait outside while she went over to the bank, said she'd be back in ten minutes. You know how long I waited out there for her?"

I falter, completely taken aback by the shards of raw pain slicing Maggie's features.

"Thirteen hours. I waited for *thirteen* hours before the

owner of the gas station finally called the cops, who carted me off to social services."

The driver pulls the golf cart to a stop in front of our bungalow, and Maggie hops out without another word. I lean in to tip the man behind the wheel, then shove my hands in the pockets of my trousers and climb the porch with slow, heavy steps. Maggie is already inside by the time I enter the room, but I still have no idea what to say to her.

Her confession reverberates through my head. It brings a knot of sickness to my stomach, a tight squeeze to my chest, and for a moment I have to wonder how this perfect night I planned ended up in shambles.

I can't wrap my brain around it. My own father walked out on me, but growing up with a warm, loving mother dulled the ache my dad's desertion left in my heart. I can't even imagine how Maggie must feel knowing she'd been abandoned on the sidewalk like a piece of trash.

"I lived in sixteen foster homes during the thirteen years I was part of the system," she says, continuing as if we'd never been interrupted. She glances at me over her shoulder, her expression unreadable. "I've been on my own since I was five years old, Ben, so don't talk to me about connections and lasting relationships. In my life, there's no such thing."

25

MAGGIE

The Gulfstream jet cruises the morning sky at thirty thousand feet, heading back in the direction of New York. But I can't decide if I'm looking forward to going home, or dreading it. Everything that happened last night still troubles me. Sonja's harsh words, the blow-up with Ben that followed. He hadn't tried to kiss or touch me after that, just slid into bed and went to sleep, while I lay awake half the night and thought about what I said to him.

My head tells me that relying on others is a mistake. But my heart speaks differently. My heart argues that I shouldn't allow the past to affect my future. That sooner or later I'll need to lower the walls I've raised and let someone in.

It's funny, really. I tried to explain to Ben why I was keeping him at arm's length, and in the process I ended up doubting my own convictions. I've always told myself I need to build my career before thinking about relationships and babies, but now I'm not so sure.

Am I using my goals as an excuse not to get close to someone? What about when I earn my degree and start that career? Will I finally open my heart and seek out love, or will I just find another goal to fixate on as a means of avoidance?

Those are questions I've never asked myself before, and I find it ironic that a cocky movie star was the one to spur this internal investigation. Celebrities are supposed to be superficial, preoccupied with material things and trivial bullshit, and although it shames me to admit it, that's partly what attracted me to Ben in the first place. I assumed he'd get bored of me after a day or two and then be on his way. The fact that he's still here is probably the most confusing thing of all.

Leaning back in my chair, I reach up to rub my temples, excruciatingly aware of Ben's presence.

Sitting there in a black long-sleeved shirt and black jeans, with morning stubble dotting his chin and dark hair falling onto his forehead, he looks sexy and dangerous. Which only reminds me of how attracted I am to him. But he hasn't said a word since we boarded the jet, and the silence between us has dragged on for so long I have no clue how to make it go away.

I don't know what to say to him. I don't know how I feel about him, and I'm not good with uncertainties.

"Gretchen was the other woman."

My head jerks up. "What?"

"Remember I said my father ran off with another woman? Well, it was Gretchen Goodrich."

I have no idea how to respond to that. So, as usual, I take the easy route. "Oh."

Ben shifts in his seat, crosses one leg over the other and inhales deeply. He looks as troubled as I feel, and I resist the urge to lean over and kiss his troubles away. That would probably be inappropriate, anyway, considering the bomb he just dropped.

"My father was always looking for a get-rich scheme,

according to my mom. And after she got pregnant, he searched for any reason to get away from her," Ben says flatly. "Spending the rest of his life in Cobb Valley, stuck with a wife and a kid, didn't appeal to him. So he made excuses to leave—phony business trips, visits to non-existent relatives. Apparently he met Gretchen during a trip to Vegas. She was nineteen at the time, vacationing with her family."

I pause. "The Hunters, right? I read online that they own a salad dressing empire or something."

"You read right." Ben's mouth twists in a wry smile. "I'm sure that's what attracted my father to her in the first place."

"So they got together?"

"They got married," he corrects.

My jaw drops. "But wasn't he already married to your mom?"

"Yup. Dear old Dad neglected to tell his new bride that he'd already tied the knot with someone else."

"What happened?" I'm utterly fascinated by this soap opera.

"Long story short, Gretchen and my father were married for two years before her parents finally stepped in. They weren't pleased with the marriage to begin with, but once my father tried to control the trust fund Gretchen received when she turned twenty-one, her father did some digging and found out about my mother and me. They had him arrested."

"For...bigamy?"

"Theft, actually. When the truth came out that his marriage to Gretchen wasn't legal, he tried to run off with a wad of cash and some of her jewelry. He was behind bars for a few years." Ben shakes his head sadly. "He had a heart attack in prison and died."

"Did you and your mother know about Gretchen?"

"Mom did, but she never told me, and the Hunters made sure to keep the scandal under wraps. I only found out when Gretchen contacted me six months ago. She was diagnosed with breast cancer, and she'd been thinking about her life, her past. She said she'd never stopped feeling guilty for being the reason my dad abandoned his family. I guess that's why she wrote me into her will."

Ben picks up his coffee cup and takes a long sip. Then he glances over with a pained expression. He looks so solemn and downcast, that this time I don't stop myself from reaching over and touching him. I squeeze his hand and interlace our fingers.

"Why didn't you just tell the truth?" I ask. "To the press, I mean?"

His fingers tighten over mine. "I thought about it, but there was my mom to consider."

"What do you mean?"

"Gretchen left me that fortune to ease her own guilt, but to me it's just a reminder of what a fucking asshole my father was. Money isn't going to make the memories go away, especially for Mom." Ben lets out a strangled groan. "Fuck, just knowing the money will be released over to me after Gretchen's estate goes through probate makes me feel like I'm betraying my mom. Like I'm profiting from her pain."

The vulnerability etched on his features leaves me speechless. How is this the same man who practically ordered me to give him a place to stay? How is this the same man whose arrogance drives me crazy?

"Not to mention," he goes on, "if I tell the media the truth about Gretchen and me, the vultures will camp out on my mom's doorstep and demand to know how she feels about her bigamist husband leaving her for an heiress. I can't do that to her." He shrugs. "Let the press think what they want of me, as long as they leave my mother alone."

I stop fighting myself and lean forward to plant a soft kiss on his lips.

"What was that for?" Ben murmurs after I pull back.

I sigh. "That was for being far more decent than I gave you credit for."

26

BEN

The second we step out of the gate at the airport, I spot the reporters.

Rather than the usual folks waiting for their friends and families, Maggie and I are greeted by a crowd of vultures with microphones and cameras. Angry flashbulbs explode in front of my eyes. A slew of questions assaults my ears.

I swallow back the rage and glance over at Maggie, who looks startled. Her green eyes widen as the mob closes in on us. "What the..."

"Move," I order before she can finish the shocked sentence.

I take her arm and practically drag her toward the exit. The press stays on our heels, capturing our every move with those intrusive cameras. We're in a large open space but I suddenly feel like the entire airport is closing in on me, and so I quicken my strides. But I loosen my grip on Maggie's arm when I notice my knuckles have turned white and are digging into her skin.

"Enjoy your vacation, Ben?" one obnoxious paparazzo calls out.

Another follows up with, "Maggie, how long have you two been seeing each other?"

How the fuck do they know her name? Without pausing to question the reporter, I push Maggie through the automatic doors. Her eyes are still wide, but she doesn't say a word. Just glances back at the vultures still buzzing around us, her expression flickering with disbelief. She looks dazed, and I don't blame her. I got used to this bullshit years ago, but I understand how it could be overwhelming for someone else.

I pull her toward a taxi, wait for her to get in, then slide inside and slam the door. Another flash catches my eye and I almost give the finger to the asshole who snapped our picture.

Leaning back in my seat, I open my mouth to address the driver, only to be cut off by Maggie. I'm taken aback when she softly gives out directions to the Olive Martini.

I frown. "Are you sure you want to go to work?"

"I don't have a choice," she says weakly. "My shift starts in an hour."

Silence stretches between us. Maggie keeps her gaze glued to the window, but I can tell she's still shaken up and confused by what just happened. I'm pretty fucking confused myself. How did the vultures learn Maggie's identity? I hadn't told a soul that I was staying at her apartment. Not even Stu or my publicist know about her. And the resort would never release the information—Marcus Holtridge and his staff respect their guests' privacy far too much to sell them out to the media, especially since the resort caters to important figures and prides itself on discretion.

Unless it wasn't a staff member who'd said anything, but another guest...

I stifle a groan as it hits me. Sonja. It had to be Sonja. She was undeniably pissed when I left her in the casino after she offended Maggie, and I wouldn't put it past my ex-fling to get even by talking to a couple of paps. Sonja knows much I hate the vultures. If she wanted revenge for my rejecting her, calling the press would be right up her alley.

The silence in the cab drags on so long I begin to feel claustrophobic again. I want to say something, but I fear anything I say will only push Maggie farther away. She was so happy and relaxed when I first brought her to the Bahamas. I know she'd been having a good time, at least up until we ran into Sonja. But despite her shutting down afterward, she'd seemed to come around again on the plane, when I told her the truth about Gretchen. I could swear we reached some kind of turning point, although I can't quite put a label on it yet. And now it's all blown to hell, thanks to a few nosy reporters.

I want to tell her I'll fix this, that somehow I'll make the media storm go away, but I know better than to make empty promises. The press will hound me no matter what I do, and even if Stu and my PR team manage to spin the story in a way that makes my relationship with Maggie not seem so tawdry, the reporters already know her name. And that means they'll soon learn everything else about her. Where she works, where she lives.

And if I know the vultures, they won't hesitate to make Maggie's life as miserable as they've made mine.

Fuck.

27

MAGGIE

"*Y*ou're late."

My head snaps up, my hand poised over the laces of my sneakers. In the doorway of the employee lounge, Lynda stands with her arms crossed over her chest. I can tell from the look on my manager's face that she isn't happy with me.

"I know, I'm sorry," I burst out, quickly kicking off my shoes and grabbing for the heels at the bottom of my locker. "It won't happen again."

"It'd better not." With a deep frown, Lynda stalks off.

Ouch.

I glance at my watch, which confirms what I already know, that my shift only started five minutes ago. Since when does Lynda get so crabby over five measly minutes?

I would've arrived at the Olive sooner, but Ben and I got stuck in traffic on the way back from the airport. And boy, had that been one awkward cab ride.

We hadn't said one word to each other, though I know it was more my fault than his. After being barraged by those reporters at the airport—reporters who knew my *name*—I didn't know what to say or how to react. The cameras, the photographers, the questions...it was all too overwhelming. Terrifying, if I'm being honest. So I'd stayed silent, despite the fact that Ben looked desperate to talk about what happened.

Well, I'm not ready to talk about it. Not now. Not when I have an entire evening of serving to get through, and when I still can't put into words how the sight of those reporters had made me feel.

Smothering a sigh, I finish dressing and tie my hair into a ponytail. God, I don't want to be here right now. How can I possibly focus on work when my body still feels bruised from all those nosy questions, and my mind is still swimming with confusion over my feelings for Ben?

The last thing I feel like doing is working, a feeling that only strengthens when I step out of the lounge and realize the owner of the bar has finally decided to make an appearance. I give a startled gasp when I bump into Jeremy Henderson in the hallway.

"Mr. Henderson, hello," I say quickly, struggling to tie my apron and keep a polite smile on my face at the same time.

He appraises me with a cool look. "You're late, Ms. Reilly."

"I know. It won't happen again," I say for the second time.

Without replying, he moves past me and rounds the counter, where he exchanges a few words with the bartenders.

I stifle another sigh. Great start to a shift—pissing off both my manager and the bar owner in less than the five minutes I was late by. I grab an order pad and a tray, and turn around just in time to bump into Trisha.

Wait—Trisha?

"Hey! What are you doing here?" I demand. "Aren't you supposed to be at the puppet show? That's why you took my shift yesterday, right?"

Splotches of crimson stain her cheeks. "Uh, I traded shifts

with Kate. Lou cancelled tonight, but we're going out to dinner tomorrow so I needed Kate to cover for me."

"Lou cancelled?"

"Yeah."

Disbelief and suspicion battle for my brain's attention. This whole shift switcheroo hasn't sat right with me from the beginning. "There was no musical, was there?" I say slowly.

Trisha's cheeks grow redder. "No," she finally admits. "But Lou and I really are going out tomorrow and it's the first time he's wanted to take me out to dinner in ages, so I had to switch with Kate and—"

"I need to speak to both of you," our manager interrupts. Lynda sharply gestures for us to follow her to the other end of the counter. With Mr. Henderson out of earshot, she fixes both of us with a deadly stare. "I spend two hours every week writing up a damn schedule, coordinating everyone's day offs, vacation requests, sick days—and I *won't* have my employees screwing around with it at their leisure."

Trisha's flush deepens. "Lynda—"

"Let me finish." She turns to me. "The next time you decide to take a personal day, you clear it with me first, understand? You don't call Trisha and Kate and make changes to the schedule without speaking to me."

I swallow. "I..."

"And you," Lynda cuts in, turning to Trisha. "You don't take anyone's shift without asking me. Now, both of you, get to work. Jeremy is here, so you'd better be on your best behavior."

"What the hell is going on?" I demand after our manager marches away. "You never cleared it with Lynda?"

"You can thank me later," Trisha shoots back. "I just got bitched at by our boss so you could go on a romantic getaway with Tony."

Tony?

Trisha hurries off before I can respond. Since I'm fairly certain my manager's eyes are glued to me, I grip my order pad and head toward one of my booths. I have to repeat my customer's order three times before I get it right, but I can't force my bewildered brain to focus.

Trisha thinks I went away with Tony? Why would she think that? And how does she even know I was away?

I drift back to the counter and place my drink orders with Matt, then curl my hands into fists as it dawns on me.

Ben.

Somehow, Ben must have contacted Trisha and asked her to cover last night's shift.

A slow rush of anger fills my veins. Damn him. When I agreed to give him a place to stay, I only asked for *one* thing in return—that he didn't complicate my life.

And what has he done? He's complicated my freaking life!

Distracted me from my schoolwork. Stuck his nose into my job. And now, thanks to him, my face will most likely be splashed on every tabloid on the news rack. The attention at the airport made me feel angry and exposed, and although I know it isn't Ben's fault the media was waiting for us in the gate, I still blame him just a little. I should've never gotten involved someone like him.

What the hell was I thinking?

My hands tremble from embarrassment as I realize that by now the entire world probably knows about me and Ben. What if the reporters start harassing me the way they harass Ben? What if they show up here at work, or my apartment, or the Broger Center? What if they dig around in my background and decide to paint me as some abandoned foster-kid gold-digger who's just after Ben Barrett's oodles of cash?

The final thought makes my hands shake harder, which causes the tray I'm holding to tilt over. The pint glasses on it slide to the edge, screwing up the balance, and before I can stop it, four tall glasses of Heineken smash onto floor.

Everything shatters, cold liquid splashing against my ankles. I blush like a tomato when I notice the entire bar has gone dead silent. Customers peer over from their booths and tables to examine what caused the enormous commotion. I turn my head away from the curious stares, and a second later I'm on my knees, fumbling for shards of glass with my bare hands.

A strong arm pushes me out of the way. "Careful, you'll cut yourself," Matt says anxiously. He's brought a rag with him and begins soaking up the spilled liquid.

"I'll clean it," I say, mortified by my clumsiness.

He pushes my hands away again. "Go clean yourself up. There's beer dripping down your legs, Mags."

"Let me help—"

"I can handle it."

He looks annoyed with me and I don't blame him. I just made a huge mess and I feel terrible that Matt is the one cleaning it up.

I swallow, nod, and rise to my feet. I spot Trisha by the counter, watching me with concern as I hurry toward the employee lounge. But my friend doesn't follow me, most likely because she doesn't want to make any more waves with Lynda.

There's a small bathroom in the back of the lounge, and I head for it, pulling paper towels out of the dispenser and wiping down my beer-soaked ankles. When I exit the bathroom, I see Jeremy Henderson striding into the lounge.

"What the hell was that?" he booms.

His harsh voice sends a cold knot of dread to my gut. The tall, balding man is absolutely seething as he approaches, tailed by Lynda, whose expression displays both worry and disapproval.

"Are you all right?" she surprises me by asking. At least one of them is concerned about my well-being.

"I'm fine. I...I'm sorry, it was an accident," I say shakily. "I lost my grip and..." I drift off, hating the pleading note in my voice. "It won't happen again."

"Damn right it won't happen again," Henderson snaps back. "You're fired."

I stumble backwards. "What? You're firing me because I dropped a tray?"

His features harden. "I'm firing you for being unable to conduct yourself in a professional manner." He lifts his hand to tick off each point with his fingers. "You've been late on more than one occasion. You changed the weekly schedule to suit your own personal needs. And you just caused a scene in front of a room full of customers. Clean out your locker, Ms. Reilly."

"Mr. Henderson—" I protest.

"Jeremy," Lynda starts with a frown.

He interrupts both of us. "Don't argue with me. The bar has already been getting bad reviews after the menu overhaul, and the scene out there did not help the Olive Martini's reputation. You no longer work for this establishment, Ms. Reilly. Is that understood?"

I blink back the hot tears prickling my eyes. "Understood," I mutter.

"Good. Now clean out your locker."

28

MAGGIE

Normally I'm home from the Olive in the wee hours of the morning. Tonight, I walk through the door at ten o'clock.

Ben's lounging on the couch watching TV. His head pops in at my entrance. "Hey," he says in surprise. "Why are you home so early? Did—shit, are you crying?"

"No," I lie stupidly. I'm visibly teary-eyed.

In a flash, he's off the couch and across the room. "Hey, don't cry," he says roughly, pulling me into his arms. "It's okay, Red."

"It's not okay." Gulping back more tears, I allow myself a few seconds of being surrounded by Ben's strong arms. Then I ease out of his embrace. "I got fired tonight."

"What?" he exclaims.

"The owner of the bar fired me."

"What? Why?"

I can't help the bite in my tone. "Messing with everyone's shifts, for one."

The guilt that fills his blue eyes confirms my earlier suspicions. Ben *was* behind Trisha's game of Musical Shifts.

"Fuck," he mumbles. He clears his throat. "Babe. I have something I need to tell—"

"I already know." I pin him down with a hard look. "You got Trisha to take my shift so we could go to the Bahamas." My mean expression doesn't last, as a weary sigh floats out. "Don't worry, your little trick wasn't the only reason I was let go. I've been late a couple times. Oh, and I dropped a tray."

He looks dumbfounded. "You dropped a tray."

"Yep. Broke a couple of glasses, spilled some beer on the floor."

"You were fired for that?"

"To quote the owner, I caused a scene."

"That son of a bitch."

More tears well up, and I give a small sniffle. "That son of a bitch was signing my paychecks. And now..." The tears spill over

"Now what?"

"Now I can't pay the rest of my tuition. I still owe the college for this semester."

"I'll pay it," Ben says instantly.

"You're *not* paying my bills." I swipe at my eyes with the sleeve of my sweater. "I'll figure out a way. Maybe the bank will give me a loan."

"Let me handle it. Please."

I gaze into his pleading eyes and shake my head. Firmly. "No, Ben."

"Goddammit, Maggie, just let me take care of you."

I bite the inside of my cheek. It's so tempting to say yes. *Take care of me. Pay my tuition so I can graduate from college. Don't ever, ever leave me.*

But the words are stuck in my throat.

"You can't do it, can you? You can't let anyone else carry

some of your burden." He exhales slowly. "Why won't you let me help?" Now he inhales. "Why won't you let me in?"

I falter. The swirl of emotion on his face is hard to process. "I..." The words escape me again. "I need a hot shower," is what I end up saying, and then I leave the room before he can object.

A few minutes later, I'm under the shower spray, letting the warm water slide over my face and ease the ache in my swollen eyes. I can't remember the last time I cried. I've always associated tears with weakness, vulnerability. And I haven't felt vulnerable since I was a child.

It bothers me that I'm crying over the loss of a stupid waitressing job. People lose their jobs all the time. It's a trivial fact of life. It isn't the end of the world.

Only it isn't trivial to me. The job at the Olive paid my bills. My savings are nonexistent, and it isn't likely I can find another job in time to pay the rest of my tuition. I'm already accruing late fees like crazy, since I didn't pay the amount in full at the beginning of the year like most students. Without my job, how am I supposed to pay the college?

I shut off the water and step out of the shower. I wrap myself up in my robe, but I hesitate before leaving the bathroom. I wonder if Ben is still in the living room. Or is he waiting in the bedroom for me? Will he start needling me again about letting him help me?

God, I don't want him to help me. But maybe I should let him. I mean, he kind of owes me, seeing as how he was partially involved in my getting fired. Why the hell did he go behind my back and mess around with my work schedule? How did he convince me to leave town for two days? Why can't he just go away?

You don't want him to go away.

I ignore the taunting voice in my head, telling myself that *of course* I want him to leave. Tonight proved that he's the complication I knew he would be, a distraction I can't afford. We have great sex, sure, but is it worth all the headaches? The reporters who surrounded us in the airport? Losing my job?

No, it isn't worth it at all. I've worked too hard to have all my goals threatened by a movie star and his amazing penis.

I stride out in my robe, determined to tell Ben it's over. That it's time for him to face the press and stop using me as an excuse to hide out. Time to uncomplicate my life. But when I enter my room and find him sitting on the bed, the speech I've prepared dies on my lips.

He looks so damn upset that my chest squeezes. His broad shoulders are slumped over, his handsome features creased with worry. And when he looks up at me, the remorse pooling in his cobalt blue eyes is unmistakable.

He stands up and says, "I'm sorry."

"Ben—"

"No, listen to me." He steps closer and touches my chin. "I'm really sorry about the way I fucked everything up. I'm sorry about the paparazzi at the airport, and I'm so fucking sorry I tricked you into going to the Bahamas with me."

Before I can speak, he kisses me, his lips softer and gentler than they've ever been. I try to focus, try to remind myself that it's time we part ways, but the feel of his hot mouth on mine is too distracting. Considering I just got fired, the last thing I should want to do is have sex, but my body instantly responds to Ben.

"Let me make it up to you," he whispers against my mouth.

I want to argue that the only way to make it up to me is to leave, to take his complications elsewhere and let me work everything out on my own. But my desire for him is too strong.

One last time, my needy body and my eager heart beg in unison.

I shouldn't listen to either of those idiots, I know that.

Falling into bed with Ben, even if it is just one last time, won't make the situation any better. I still won't have a job, the press will still be sniffing around me, Ben will still be asking me for things I'm not sure I can give. Sex isn't going to change that.

But I can't ignore my need for this man. And when his gorgeous eyes lock with mine and ask an unspoken question, I can't say no.

I nod.

Without another word, Ben leads me toward the bed and peels the robe off my body. He grabs a condom, and then he lays me down on the patterned bedspread and kisses me again. He kisses me everywhere. My lips. My nipples. My stomach, my thighs, my clit. And while his tongue teases and explores every inch of me, all my anxiety dissolves and flees my body in the form of a soft whimper.

Silently, Ben removes his own clothes and lowers his body on mine. His cock slides into me in one swift stroke, but he doesn't move, just leaves himself buried deep inside me.

Our gazes collide, and what I see steals the breath from my lungs. He looks turned on and needy and even a little vulnerable, and my heart does somersaults in my chest.

"Maggie," he says, his voice coming out hoarse, ragged.

I wait for him to continue. He doesn't. Instead he starts to move, his pace a sweet, rolling rhythm that has me gasping with impatience. He ignores my tiny whimpers, the way I grip his butt and try to pull him deeper inside.

"There's no rush," he whispers, pushing strands of hair out of my eyes.

He resumes the slow pace and I'm not sure how long he keeps it up. Minutes could've ticked by, hours even, but I don't care. My eyelids flutter closed, and I almost purr, breathing in Ben's spicy masculine scent as he fucks me slowly.

I kiss his chest, running my tongue along his collarbone,

meeting his gentle thrusts with the measured rise of my hips. And just when I'm getting close, he withdraws abruptly, slides down between my legs, and presses his lips to my swollen clit. Licking, sucking, until I cry out from an orgasm so intense a wave of dizziness crashes over me.

Ben doesn't let me recover, nor does he resume his lazy pace when he thrusts back inside me. "Now we can rush," he growls, and plunges into me so fast and deep that it isn't long before a second orgasm seizes my inner muscles. A moment later, Ben shudders and comes, finally allowing himself his own release.

He kisses my forehead, and then rolls off me to dispose of the condom. Staring at his sinewy, sweat-soaked back, I bite my lip to stop myself from asking him what just happened. Sex happened, duh, but it feels like something between us has shifted. Something that scares me and exhilarates me at the same time. Something I can't explain with words, or label, or even analyze.

Oh fuck.

For the first time in my life, I wonder if maybe I'm falling in love.

29

MAGGIE

$\mathcal{I}$ don't wake Ben before I leave the apartment the next morning. I know it makes me a coward, but I'm not ready to face him yet. Something changed last night and I know he felt it too. It showed in the way he held me after sex, the way he stroked my hair and fell asleep with his head against my breasts. The entire exchange was so damn intimate that I don't even know what to make of it. It worries me. So much that I'm sneaking out today without a word and heading to the community center despite the chicken pox risk.

I just can't be around Ben right now. Last night when the L-word floated its way into my mind, I was stunned. And terrified. Is it even possible to start falling for someone this fast? I've never been in love before, never allowed myself to feel anything even remotely close to it, so the fact that I somehow dropped my guard around Ben is petrifying. I'm supposed to hate him for messing with my job, for complicating my entire life with his sexy smiles and drugging kisses.

A day working with the kids is what I need. Kids have the strangest ability to clear your head and help you gain perspective on life.

I don't usually work on Sundays, but I need to be out of the apartment, away from Ben and the conflicting emotions he stirs inside me. Paying my driver, I step out of the car and onto the sidewalk. The temperature is surprisingly hot for May. The sky is a clear blue and the breeze warm as it snakes through my hair. Yet, despite such a perfect day, the Broger Center is under attack by an evil presence.

As in, the crowd of paparazzi milling on the sidewalk in front of the building.

A chill runs up my spine despite the sunshine warming my face. The crowd rushes me the second they spot me.

"Maggie!" one reporter shouts. "Maggie, want to say a few words to TMZ?"

Oh God.

"How long have you been dating Ben Barrett?"

"Are you aware of his affair with Gretchen Goodrich?"

I want to melt into the sidewalk and become one with the cement, but the jerks won't let me. Before I can blink, they've surrounded me. Cameras keep getting thrust in my direction.

"Maggie, did Ben pay you for sex? Is that why you were with him at the Lester Hotel?"

Something sharp pierces my heart. Are they implying I'm a *prostitute?*

Unable to breathe, I push one of the cameras out of my face and stalk forward. "I won't even dignify that with an answer," I mutter.

I zigzag through the mob, my steps getting faster the closer I get to the door. Once inside, I hurry down the corridor and wait until I'm out of sight from the front windows before I sag against the wall and gasp for air.

Why the hell is this happening? Why do these strangers even care about me?

"Maggie?"

I lift my head to find one of the counselors eyeing me with concern. "Hey, Karen," I say, my voice unsteady.

"Gloria is in her office." Karen looks hesitant. "You should probably go in and see her."

"All right."

Collecting my nerves, I walk to the main office. The teenage receptionist greets me with a sympathetic smile. An omen of things to come, obviously.

I head for my boss's open doorway. The tiny Hispanic woman behind the desk gestures for me to close the door. "Hey, Maggie. Have a seat."

I sit.

"Apparently you're something of a celebrity." Gloria's tone isn't angry, but bemused. Her gaze not accusatory, but concerned.

"Gloria...I'm so sorry about all this." I wring my hands together, lace my fingers, then unlace them and tuck my palms on my knees, but no amount of fidgeting can stop the river of guilt flowing inside me.

And I'm furious with those fucking reporters. It's Sunday morning. The kids visiting the center today don't deserve to have a bunch of slimy creeps snapping their pictures. Nobody here deserves all this unwanted attention.

"So you're dating a movie star?" Gloria offers a small smile. "To be honest, I'm not sure if I envy you or pity you. Having the media on your back must be awful."

I gulp. "Yes, it is."

"Maggie, I'm going to be honest here."

And here it comes.

"All this attention isn't good for the center."

A sigh lodges in the back of my throat. "I know." The Broger Center doesn't just give children a place to play sports, or get help with their homework. We also offer counseling services, and most of the kids—and parents—who come here are or have been victims of abuse. Sometimes we even provide shelter to women who show up having escaped from abusive husbands or boyfriends. We let them stay in one of the rooms on the third floor while we help them plan their next move.

Needless to say, this place won't be a safe haven for anyone as long as its picture is splashed all over the papers.

"None of our kids, nor their parents, deserve to be pulled into a celebrity scandal." Gloria's voice draws me from my troubled thoughts.

"I agree," I say quietly. "And I promise you I'll straighten all this out."

"I know you will." She leans forward and rests her elbows on the desk. "But, until you do, it might be a good idea for you not to come in."

My heart clenches. "If you think that's best."

"I know you wanted a permanent position here, honey, but right now isn't the time to discuss it. Why don't we let the media storm die down before we talk about anything permanent?"

Her words are like individual little stab wounds, and they leave me with a feeling of raw emptiness in my stomach. Piece by piece, my life is crumbling around me. Everything I've worked so hard for. Losing my job at the Olive was bad. Losing my place at the youth center absolutely crushes me.

"I guess I'll be in touch, then," I murmur, fighting hard to stop my tears from spilling over. I rise to my feet and extend my hand. "Thanks for being so nice about this."

Gloria shakes my hand. "This isn't personal, honey. I'm just trying to protect our community. Give me a call when things settle down, okay?"

"Sure."

I leave Gloria's office with my chin high and my shoulders stiff, but it takes all my willpower not to collapse on the linoleum floor beneath my feet. Somehow my legs manage to carry me outside, where I push through the nosy paparazzi and utter the words "no comment" so many times I want to scream.

They follow me. They actually follow me to the curb, hurling questions at me. *Ben Barrett. Gretchen Goodrich. Lester Hotel. Sex. Affair.* The words all mingle into one pounding bass line, making my head hurt.

Only when I flag down a cab and slide into the backseat do I finally allow the tears to fall.

30

BEN

I already know about the paparazzi at the Broger Center when Maggie walks into the apartment. I saw it on TMZ, and I'd never felt so powerless, not to mention enraged, at the sight of Maggie's wide, confused eyes and her expression of sheer shock when that one jackass asked if I'd paid her for sex.

The accusation leaves me sick to my stomach. Maggie does not deserve to be humiliated like that.

"Red," I start as she drops her keys on the hall table.

She silently heads for the kitchen.

I follow her, uneasy, maybe even a bit scared as I watch her pour a glass of water.

"Maggie," I prompt.

Still no answer. Face blank, she sips on her water.

"Goddammit, babe, will you talk to me?"

Her throat bobs as she swallows, her face scrunched up in disgust. "They followed me home," she says. "They're outside the building."

My fists tighten with frustration. "I'll call my agent to see how we can get rid of them."

"Don't bother."

She blows past me and settles on the living room couch, leaving me to stare after her in bewilderment. Why is she acting so calm? Her privacy is being violated, her good name slandered, and she doesn't care?

I rub my temples, unnerved by her reaction. I don't like this. I don't like the vacant look in her green eyes or the way she's brushing all this off.

"I won't let them say all this bullshit about you," I finally growl. I pace the hardwood floor, fists still clenched. "We need to put a stop to this. Maybe we can file a restraining order." But I know how unlikely that is. I've been dealing with these assholes for years. If they smell a scoop, nothing will stop them from getting it.

"Do you care about me, Ben?"

I frown.

"Do you care about me?" she repeats.

I sweep my gaze over her. She looks young and vulnerable in her blue jeans and V-neck T-shirt, her face free of makeup, her pretty features imploring me as she awaits my response. She wore her hair loose today, and it's falling down her shoulders in soft waves, straight and curly at the same time. Wild and guarded, just like Maggie.

"Of course I care about you," I say roughly. "Hell, I—" *might be falling in love with you.* But I don't say that out loud. This woman has been a flight risk from day one. Any declaration of potential love will probably send her spiraling.

"Good." She tucks a strand of hair behind her ear and our eyes lock. "Then you need to leave."

I stumble back. "What?"

"You need to leave, Ben. If you leave, they leave."

I can't believe she's saying this. Yes, my presence in her life is currently causing an enormous mess, but I can make it go away. I'm Ben Barrett, for chrissake.

That's the problem, pal.

I try to silence the harsh criticism that surfaces, but it won't go away. It won't go away because it's the truth. Maggie is right. The problem isn't whether I can get the paps to leave her alone —it's that I placed her in the spotlight to begin with. My celebrity is ruining her fucking life.

If I weren't Ben Barrett, but just a normal man with a normal life, Maggie wouldn't be suffering right now.

"Gloria asked me not to come back to the center."

Fuck. "Because of the paparazzi?" I ask, even though I already know the answer.

"Yeah." Maggie pauses. "Look, I can find another waitressing job, but I can't be a social worker if I'm being followed and hounded by reporters. It's not fair to the kids I work with."

"Maybe you can put social work on hold for a while? Just until this all dies down." I almost cringe at the desperation in my tone.

"On hold?" She casts a withering look in my direction. "It's taken me six years to finish school. Attending classes part-time so I could work to pay my own tuition, so I wouldn't be drowning in student-loan debt when I graduate. I've sacrificed friendships and relationships to keep up my schedule. I don't have a goddamn life because of it, and now you're telling me to put it on hold? That's like saying all those years of hard work meant absolutely nothing."

"I know."

"I won't throw it all away."

"I know." My throat tightens to the point where swallowing actually hurts. I know she's right. I just don't *want* her to be right.

"I don't fit into your life, Ben. You said so yourself—you live in a plastic world." She rises to her feet and eliminates the distance between us. "I can't live in a plastic world. I need my life to mean something. Especially since I felt so meaningless growing up."

Maggie reaches up and strokes my stubble-covered cheek. I haven't shaved since we returned from Nassau, and the feel of her fingertips scraping over my two-day-old beard is torture.

"You need to leave," she says again.

How perfectly ironic. I've starred in dozens of movies where I play the savior who always gets the girl, but in real life it's the exact opposite. I won't get the girl this time. And instead of saving her, I turned her entire world off-kilter.

"If you want me to go, I'll go." I choke on the bittersweet lump in my throat. "But I want to thank you first."

"For what?"

"For being there when I needed somebody." I gulp. "And for being so damn real."

Her bottom lip quivers. She blinks a couple times as if she's fighting back tears. Somehow this makes me feel slightly better, knowing that saying goodbye is as hard for her as it is for me.

With a rueful smile, I trace the seam of her lips with my thumb, then lower my head to kiss the quivering away. It's the sweetest kiss we've ever shared, and something inside me shatters when I finally pull my mouth away.

I take a step toward the front door, then pause to flash her my best Ben Barrett grin, and hope she can't hear the sound of my heart cracking open in my chest.

"Ben?"

"Yeah?"

"I'm sorry," Maggie whispers.

"Don't be. I'm the one who should be sorry." I grip the doorknob with one unsteady hand. "Goodbye, Red."

31

BEN

"The prodigal son returns!" my mother declares as I trudge into the front hallway of my childhood home.

It's nearly one in the morning, but I'm not surprised to see Mom up and about. She's the ultimate night owl. I can't even count how many times I'd slithered home in my youth at three in the morning thinking I orchestrated a successful sneak-out—only to find my mother baking cookies in the kitchen.

In fact, as I kick off my shoes and walk toward her, the scent of baked goods floats into my nostrils. Mom's long red apron and the white flour sticking to her dark hair confirm she was baking up a storm prior to my arrival.

"You should have told me you were coming to visit," my mother chides with a shake of her head. "I would've baked another batch."

"Sorry, I probably should've called." I remove my leather jacket and toss it aside, then step forward to embrace my mother.

"It's so good to see you," she says, tightly returning the hug.

I kiss the top of her head, link my arm through hers, and we stroll through the oak swivel door leading into the kitchen.

After receiving my very first million-dollar paycheck, I'd offered to buy Mom a new house, but she refused. She loves the small bungalow she raised me in, and I have to admit I like it too. It represents a warmth and coziness my life lacks these days.

"To what do I owe this visit?" It doesn't take long for my mother's blue eyes to fill with suspicion.

"Just felt like coming home, I guess." I round the counter and flop onto one of the tall white stools. "It was sort of a last-minute decision."

"Every decision you make is last-minute, Benjamin. You're nothing if not spontaneous."

Well, she has me on that one. My impulsive nature is how I ended up with Maggie. I forced my way into her apartment—and her life—without even knowing why I was doing it. And look how that turned out—I cost Maggie her job, her dreams and her privacy.

Spontaneous is often just another word for *fucking selfish*.

"So, what have you done?" Mom asks. She pours a glass of milk and sets it on the weathered cedar counter in front of me.

I frown. "What makes you think I did something?"

Chuckling, she slides two huge oven mitts on her hands and removes a tray of chocolate chip cookies from the middle rack. "You've got guilt written all over your face," she tosses over her shoulder. She sets the baking tray on the stove to cool. "And please don't tell me you got another tattoo. You have enough."

"No tattoo." I release the sigh lodged in my chest. "I met someone, Mom."

Gaping, my mother turns to face me. "Seriously?"

I nod glumly. "Seriously."

"And?"

"And I like her. I might even love her a little."

"Victoria's Secret or *Vogue*?"

"Neither. She's a civilian."

After another second of bewilderment, her eyes light up like a string of Christmas lights. As a huge grin stretches across her face, she whips off her oven mitts. "Tell me everything," she orders.

So I tell her. About Maggie. About the hotel room mishap that threw us together (though I leave out the details of what *happened* during that room mishap). I finish with the entire paparazzi mess and Maggie's request that I leave, ending with, "So basically, I screwed up her life."

Then I groan and reach for the milk in front of me, feeling like a little kid again as I sip the cold liquid.

"You didn't screw up her life," my mother soothes. "It will all settle down sooner or later."

"Yeah, until the next scandal hits. Maggie doesn't want to be part of my lifestyle. She doesn't want that kind of attention."

Mom assumes that knowing look of wisdom I've grown used to over the years. "The only reason you receive that kind of attention, sweetheart, is because you go out looking for it."

My jaw drops. "I do not."

"Sure you do." She shrugs at my indignant reaction. "You date floozies, Ben. And when you date floozies, the media likes to take pictures of you with your floozies."

"Stop saying floozies," I grumble.

"Don't sulk, sweetheart. You know I'm right. You do flashy things with flashy women."

Fine, maybe my mother has a point. There are plenty of other celebrities, actors far more famous than me, who don't find their faces splashed across the tabloids every week. I don't go out and solicit the attention, but I can see Mom's point. The women I date are gorgeous, glitzy, and demanding to be noticed. Women like Sonja, who may as well be wearing a sign that reads "NOTICE ME! TAKE MY PICTURE!"

"This Maggie sounds very down to earth," Mom says. "And

—I don't mean this as an insult—she also seems like the type who wouldn't make the media drool. They need teeny-bikini models to sell covers, not your average Jane type. She's too normal for those idiots."

I grin. "You're right about that." My expression quickly sobers. "But that doesn't take away from the fact that they're still all over me. Especially since Gretchen died."

I almost flinch, expecting to see sorrow, or maybe anger, in my mother's eyes, but she surprises me. Looking serious, she crosses her arms over her apron and says, "Tell the truth already, Ben. Tell them about Gretchen and your father."

My eyebrows shoot up. "Are you kidding? I'd never do anything to embarrass you, Mom."

She rolls her eyes. "You're embarrassing me now, for God's sake! Everyone in town thinks my son goes to bed with women twice his age—for money! The other day Susan pulled me aside in the pharmacy and suggested you go into therapy."

I can't help but laugh. "You're lying."

"Nope. Call Susan yourself. I'm sure she has a list of shrinks written up."

"So you honestly don't care if I tell the world that Dad was a bigamist and a thief?"

"Of course not." Her features soften. "Sweetheart, I've come to terms with what your father did. In fact, I came to terms with it a long time ago. You don't need to protect me from it."

I hesitate. "What about the money?"

"What about it?"

"I don't feel right keeping it," I confess.

"Then give it away." Mom shrugs. "There are lots of deserving charities out there, and if Gretchen's money is that much of a burden for you, donate it."

As usual, my mother is nothing if not frank. She's always been frank. Always been the strongest woman I've ever known, too, which makes me wonder why I ever believed she'd be embarrassed or ashamed if the truth about my connection to Gretchen came out.

"Now, about Maggie," she continues, strolling back to the stove to pluck one cookie from the tray. "I assume you'll do everything you can to get her back?"

A faint smile plays on my lips. Then I nod. "You assume right."

32

MAGGIE

*T*wo days after I sent Ben away, I still haven't mastered the art of getting off the couch and changing out of my ratty old sweats. Tough. I don't feel like getting up or brushing my hair or pretending that I'm anything but what I currently feel: miserable.

It's not like I have a job to go to, anyway. No school either, since my first exam isn't until next week. And although most of the reporters have abandoned their stakeout of the Broger Center, a few overly ambitious ones still linger, making me feel uneasy about going back. Sooner or later I'll call Gloria and talk about that permanent position. But not today.

"Jeez, Maggie, did you rob a bank?" comes my roommate's incredulous cry.

I twist my head in time to see Summer walk in, looking tanned, healthy and seriously confused. In comparison, I feel like a mess with my tangled hair and wrinkled clothing. A big, pathetic mess.

"Yes, Summer, I robbed a bank," I say dryly.

Eyeing my disheveled appearance, Summer drops her bright red suitcase and marches toward the couch. "Seriously, why are there reporters standing outside our building? I heard one of them quizzing the security guard about you. Are you in trouble?"

"I guess you could say that." I release a heavy sigh. "I did something stupid."

"Do I even want to know?"

"I fell in love with a movie star."

Summer's stunned silence doesn't come as any surprise. Hell, I was pretty stunned myself when I figured it out. The night Ben left, I went to bed alone. And when I was lying there in the dark, staring up at the ceiling, I came to a realization that rendered any chance of falling asleep impossible.

I realized that the ache in my heart, and the empty feeling in my stomach, and the unbearable weight bearing down on my chest...it had nothing to do with losing my job.

And everything to do with losing Ben.

"How long have I been gone for?" Summer demands, blinking wildly. "In a week and a half you managed to fall in love with a movie star? Is this a joke?"

"Nope. It's true."

She motions for me to move over, then flops down beside me. "Okay, spill."

"Remember my stranger?"

"Of course."

"Turns out he's Ben Barrett—"

"Ben Barrett the actor?" Summer exclaims.

I stare at her. "Yes. As in, I fell for a stupid movie star."

"Oh gosh, he is *hot*. Plus his movies have a ton of explosions, so Tygue doesn't complain about watching them. It's win-win."

"Not for me," I mumble. Then, in a shaky voice, I recap all the events that Summer missed when she was away.

"Holy shit," she breathes when I finish. "You lost your job? I'm so sorry."

I shrug. "It wasn't your fault."

"I know, but—"

My ringing cell phone cuts her off. A tiny pang of hope tugs at my insides, but I will it away. It won't be Ben. I asked him to leave. He hasn't called since and he won't call now.

A quick glance at the screen tells me I'm right. The caller is Tony, of all people.

I furrow my brow and answer the call, mostly out of curiosity. I haven't heard from Tony since he left that message apologizing for the hotel room mix-up. "Hey, Tony," I greet him.

"Maggie! I've got good news, babe. I'll be in the city tomorrow night."

He'll be in the city? I almost laugh out loud, realizing how things have changed so dramatically since the last time I spoke to—or thought about—Tony. A few weeks ago, I would've jumped up and down with excitement at the sound of his voice, at the idea of meeting up and going to bed with him. Now, it's the last thing I want. How can I just forget everything that happened and go back to the way I was in the pre-Ben days? How can I ever settle for casual sex when I experienced something deeper?

"That's great," I answer, my tone hardly enthusiastic.

"Don't sound so thrilled about it," he teases.

"I'm sorry. I just...I've met someone." Next to me, Summer's eyebrows shoot up to her hairline.

There's a brief silence. "You're kidding me," Tony finally says, chuckling softly.

I bristle. "It's not funny."

"I'm not making fun of you, babe. I'm just amazed. What happened to the Maggie I meet three times a year?"

"Two times," I correct.

"Is it serious?" Tony asks.

I draw in a breath. "Yeah. I think so. I'm sorry."

"Hey, don't apologize. We had a good run, right?"

"It was great," I say, and I mean it. My casual trysts with Tony *were* great. But I don't want great anymore. I want incredible. I want body-numbing. Toe-curling. Heart-thumping.

I want Ben.

As my eyes well up with unwelcome tears, I utter a quick goodbye and hang up, swiping at my damp lashes with the sleeve of my sweatshirt. Damn it. I'm sick of crying.

"This is why I never wanted anything serious," I complain. "Feeling miserable sucks." I run my hands through my messy hair and release a groan.

Summer stares at me. "You're a different person. How the hell did this happen?"

I manage a faint smile. "I'm still the same person."

"I'm serious, Mags. You just broke it off with *Tony*. Tony, for God's sake! The guy you can't wait to see each time he comes to visit."

"I guess Two-Time Tony isn't enough anymore," I admit. "Ben...well, he made me realize something. I...don't want to be alone." Saying those words out loud is difficult. But cathartic, too, because they're undeniably true. The past few days without Ben have been horrible. Miserable and horrible and excruciatingly lonely.

The loneliness is what finally got to me. For so long I've worked my ass off to make something of myself. I wanted my life to mean something, I wanted to matter, if only to the kids I worked with, and that's what drove me. Saving money, getting a college degree, finding a meaningful job. But what happens afterwards? What happens when I go home at night—alone? When I wake up every morning—alone? When the only person I'm able to share my dreams, thoughts and feelings with is a roommate who'll soon be building her own life with the man she loves?

I'll have a career, I'll spend my afternoons doing something meaningful, but what's the point if I don't have anyone to share it with?

"I miss him," I bleakly tell Summer. "I miss talking to him and joking around with him. I miss kissing him. Hell, I even miss listening to him sing along to the Beach Boys."

A knowing smile curves her mouth. "It's a pretty amazing feeling, isn't it? Being in love?" She pauses. "And, listen, I know this probably isn't the time to tell you this, but...Tygue and I are getting married."

For a moment, all my problems whisk out of my tired brain. "Really?"

Summer blushes. "He proposed on the last night of our trip. We're thinking a Christmas wedding in Jamaica."

"Oh my God! Really?" I sling my arm over her shoulder and squeeze her warmly. "I'm so happy for you guys. Congratulations."

"Thanks." She pauses again. "Why don't you call him?"

"Tygue? I can just congratulate him in person."

"Not Tygue. Ben."

"I can't call him."

"Why not?"

"Because I asked him to leave."

"So ask him to come back."

I swallow. "It's not that simple. Look, even if I do tell him how I feel, the media won't stop harassing us. And as long as the press is interested in me, Gloria won't let me work at the center."

Summer's expression softens. "Then you need to ask yourself this—what's more important to you: your job or Ben?"

"C'mon, don't make this about me having to choose."

"What if that's what it comes down to?"

I grow silent. What if it did come to that? I'm not sure what

I'd do. I want to be with Ben, but I'm not ready to give up everything I worked so hard for either.

And what if I do decide Ben is worth being hounded by the paparazzi and risking my job for? If we end up breaking up someday, I'll be left with nothing. I'll be no better than my mother, a woman who left her responsibilities at a gas station in Queens for a man and a relationship that, knowing my mother's flakiness, probably hadn't even worked out.

Does my mother regret leaving me? This isn't the first time I've wondered, and it probably won't be the last, but it's the question that always keeps me in line, urging me to make something of myself.

"I don't want to talk about this anymore," I grumble, too confused to think. "Tell me about your trip. How did the steel drum performance go? Did you get along with Tygue's family?"

After a beat, Summer grants me the change the subject. "His family *loved* me. And everyone at the reception gave me a standing ovation after I finished my song."

I snort. "Uh-huh. Now that's something I've got to see to believe."

She smiles smugly. "Luckily for you, Tygue got it all on tape."

33

BEN

"*B*en, have a seat," Alan Goodrich says after we enter the spacious living room of his Beverly Hills mansion.

I assume a relaxed demeanor and sink onto the black leather sofa situated in front of a forbidding stone fireplace. I'd visited the Goodrich home only once before, when Gretchen first contacted me six months ago, but the opulent surroundings still make me a little uncomfortable. Hell, just being in Alan's presence makes me uncomfortable. The man is one of the most esteemed directors in the business, recipient of two Oscars, not to mention a list of nominations and critic nods as long as the Nile.

I'm still not sure why Alan wanted to meet with me, but I hope it doesn't have to do with Gretchen.

Of course it has to do with Gretchen. Why else would he ask you to come?

"So. Ben. Why don't we skip the pleasantries and get right down to business?" Alan announces. "I have two matters to discuss."

"Okay."

I'm feeling unnerved. With his barrel chest, shock of white hair, and piercing eyes, Alan Goodrich is nothing if not intimidating. Lowering his beefy body into a leather recliner, he folds his hands in his lap. "First, you should know that my wife's estate has been settled. Since the will was uncontested, you should receive a check very soon."

I swallow. "About that...I don't feel comfortable keeping Gretchen's money, Mr. Goodrich."

"Call me Alan."

"Okay. Alan. I've decided to donate the money to charity. I got a few organizations in mind, but if Gretchen had any pet causes, let me know and I'll be sure to make a donation."

He nods. "I'll have my assistant send you a list."

"Also...I wanted to ask you something. I'd like to give a statement to the press about Gretchen's connection to my father."

Alan grows silent.

"That is, if you don't mind," I add quickly.

"Actually, I think it's a fine idea." His strong, somewhat harsh features soften. "Gretchen would've hated it if she knew your inheritance caused a media circus. She really did feel awful about what your father did to you and your mother. I don't think she would've ever written you into her will if she knew the kind of negative attention you'd receive."

"I know." From what I knew of her, Gretchen had a big heart.

"So clear it up, son. It's about time the press cut you some slack."

"Thanks, Alan."

He gives a brisk nod. "Now, to the second matter at hand. I don't know if you've heard, but I'm currently working on a World War Two picture."

"I'd heard, yes."

"We're scouting locations and beginning to cast as we speak."

I cross my ankles together, suddenly remembering the advice Maggie gave me in Nassau. *Nobody's going to give it to you. If you want something, you go after it.*

I'm not sure where Goodrich is heading or why he mentioned his latest film, but I know I can't allow the opportunity to slip through my fingers. Maggie was right. I can't sit around and wait for a meaty role to fall into my lap. If I want it, I need to *take* it.

"About this project..." I venture quietly. "I was actually going to ask you if you'd let me read for it."

The director chuckles. "Ben—"

I try not to bristle at his laughter and hurry on. "I'm not asking for a leading role, Alan. I'll read for any part you want, as small as you want."

"Ben—"

"Just give me a shot."

"That's exactly what I intend to do," he says, chuckling again. "If you had let me finish, you would have heard me offering you one of the supporting roles."

My jaw falls open despite my attempt to keep it shut. "Are you fucking with me?"

Alan offers a faint smile. "Don't look so shocked. I've told you before how much I enjoy your performances."

"Yeah, but I thought..." I trail off.

"You thought I was bullshitting?" he finishes. His smile widens. "I wasn't. And the moment I finished reading this latest script, I knew I wanted you to be in the film."

Before I can answer, a mechanical rendition of a Beethoven symphony breaks out. With an apologetic look, Goodrich reaches into the inner pocket of his navy-blue blazer and extracts a razor-thin phone. "Excuse me for a moment. I need to take this."

As he exits the room, I rub my forehead, still a little stunned. Alan Goodrich just offered me a role in his new movie? Sure, it's a war epic, so there's bound to be action, the gunfire and explosions I've grown used to, but there'll also be *depth* to it. Not to mention the respect and prestige that comes from working with a director of Alan's caliber. Just having my name attached to a Goodrich project will certainly make the critics take notice, even if I am Bad Boy Ben Barrett.

Hell, maybe they'll finally drop the "bad boy" and see me simply as Ben Barrett, actor.

"I'm going to have to cut this meeting short," comes Goodrich's rueful voice. The director stands in the doorway, still holding his cell phone.

I walk toward Alan and extend my hand. "Not a problem. I've got somewhere to be anyway."

He gives a firm handshake. "We'll start shooting at the end of the summer. My team will be in touch with your agent this week. Sound good?"

"Sounds great."

I leave the Goodrich estate feeling like I'm walking on air. An enormous weight has lifted off my chest, the weight of discontent and frustration over a career that strayed off in a direction I never wanted. But it's back on track again, and soon the other pieces of my life will fall into place.

First things first, though. I have a press conference to attend.

34

MAGGIE

*I*t's early morning when I approach the front steps of the youth center and spot a half-dozen reporters milling about. The sight makes me frown. Don't these people have lives? Homes to go to? Kids to take care of? Don't they have anything better to do than to stalk a nobody like me?

Fortunately, I finally showered and changed my clothes, but I'm pretty sure I still look haggard. I didn't sleep a wink last night. I haven't been sleeping in general. It's impossible to when I miss Ben and am swamped with regret about asking him to leave.

But yesterday, after lying in bed until two a.m., I finally decided enough was enough. I reached for the phone to call him, only to realize I don't have his fucking phone number. We never had any need for texts or phone calls, because he was living in my damn apartment.

So I dragged Summer out of bed to help me search online, and although we spent hours looking for a contact number, all we got was a fan mail address. When we finally hit pay dirt and learned the name of Ben's agent, it was too late to call or email the agency. Which meant another sleepless night, leading to a crappy morning when I rolled my exhausted body out of bed and heard Gloria's voicemail asking me to come in for another meeting.

And now, seeing all these stupid reporters on the front steps only makes my bad mood a hundred times worse.

"Did you know Ben was donating a quarter of his inheritance to the Broger Center?" one of the reporters shouts as I approach.

I stop for a second. What the hell is this guy talking about?

"Maggie," someone else calls. "Were you aware that Ben's father was a bigamist?"

Huh?

Not bothering to respond, I walk inside and immediately head for the main office, my mind swimming. How did they find out about Ben's father? And what on earth do they mean he donated his inheritance to the center?

"Maggie, I'm glad you came in!" Gloria chirps when I enter her office.

Her expression is so jubilant that my confusion doubles. I settle in the visitor's chair and try to paste on a cheerful expression. "Hey, Gloria." My attempt at a smile doesn't last long. "I take it the reporters are still harassing everyone?"

She waves a dismissive hand. "They'll go away eventually."

My eyebrows shoot upward. Was I transported to a different planet during the night? A few days ago, Gloria was pissed off about the media presence. Today, she seems totally unperturbed and relaxed about the entire situation.

"One of the reporters outside mentioned Ben donated some money to the center?" I ask, feeling awkward about my ignorance on the subject.

Gloria's dark eyes light up. "Five million dollars is not *some money*, sweetheart. I'm still stunned by Mr. Barrett's generosity."

Five million dollars?

"I must say, I'm impressed with the man. That he donated more than half of his recent inheritance to various child service agencies across the country is commendable, but giving such a substantial amount to this center? It's unbelievably generous."

"I can't believe he did this," I murmur. Then I realize something. "But...Gloria, Ben's donation means that the reporters won't be going away for a while."

Her face softens, remorse reflecting in her gaze. "Maggie, I may have overreacted during our last meeting. My biggest concern at the time was what the attention would do to the center, not to mention how the parents would feel." She shakes her head in amusement. "Turns out most of them are thrilled by the free publicity."

"They are?"

Gloria nods whole-heartedly. "Many of them feel this will be good for the community, maybe spur the city counselors to take notice of what's happening outside their offices. And now, thanks to Mr. Barrett's generosity, we'll be able to bring about a lot of changes." She leans forward on her elbows, her expression growing excited. "This money will allow us to completely renovate the center. We're planning on building a new playground and an on-site tutoring center for kids with learning problems."

"What about the women who come here to escape abusive situations? How will they feel about the attention?"

"That's the best part. We're going to use a portion of the money to build a women's shelter, in a separate location. More space, more counselors, it'll be wonderful."

I'm speechless. Considering my last meeting with Gloria, I hadn't expected her to be so pleased about the turn of events. "So you're okay with the media hanging around?" I ask warily.

"I don't have much of a choice," she replies with a dry smile.

"With a donation this size, it's expected. Besides, it really is good publicity, which is something I failed to consider when we spoke last time."

I sigh softly. "Well, I'm glad something good came out of all this."

"Something terrific, you mean," Gloria corrects. "And I forgot to mention—we're going to offer after-school workshops for the kids. Drama, music, art. In fact, we just hired someone. He'll be working with the kids all summer."

"That's wonderful."

She rises from her chair. "I'd like you to meet him."

"You would?"

Catching my mystified expression, she offers a slight smile. "Humor me, will you?"

"Sure." I stand up and follow Gloria out of the small office toward the main corridor. Most of the rooms in the Broger Center are miniscule, but we do have a large indoor gymnasium the kids use during the winter and on rainy days. Gloria leads me in the direction of the gym, and we pause in front of the splintered double doors.

"Also, I'd like to speak to you afterward about that permanent position," she says casually.

My heart soars. "Really?"

She smiles. "You're going to be a fantastic addition and a huge asset to these kids, Maggie."

I expect Gloria to enter the gym first, but the woman simply opens the door and gestures for me to go in. "You're not coming?" I say in surprise.

"Nah." Gloria gives a quick shrug. "I already got his autograph."

His autograph?

"Wait—who exactly am I meeting?" I ask.

"The new drama teacher," she chirps before strolling away.

Baffled, I walk into the gym—and stop in my tracks when I lay eyes on Ben.

"Hey, Red," he calls, his deep voice bouncing off the gymnasium walls.

I gulp. God, he looks good. He's clad in a pair of faded blue jeans, a snug black T-shirt, and combat boots. He's shaved since the last time I saw him, but his chiseled face still possesses its usual bad-boy sexiness, and his perfectly shaped lips look so damn kissable I shiver.

"What are you doing here?" I squeak.

He crosses the waxed floor with lazy strides, and each step he takes quickens my pulse. When he's finally standing in front of me, my heart is thudding against my ribs and pounding in my ears.

"I'm going to be teaching a free acting workshop here for the summer," he replies with a charming smile.

I stare at him. "Why?"

He shrugs. "Because I have the summer off. I figured it would be fun."

"I mean, why *here*?" I stammer. "I'm sure thousands of people would pay big bucks for an acting class with you."

"Haven't you learned by now that I don't care about money?"

I don't even know how to respond. A hundred questions bite at my tongue, but I force myself not to ask them. Quizzing Ben about his donation or his presence here doesn't matter right now. Not when we have more important things to say. Not when *I* have something important to say.

"I'm sorry I asked you to leave," I blurt out.

"You had every right to." He reaches out and strokes my cheek with the pad of his thumb.

I hold my breath, waiting for him to pull me toward him,

anticipating his kiss. But it doesn't come. Instead, his features crease with remorse and his hand drops to his side.

"I made a mess of your life, babe. I don't blame you for asking me to go." His Adam's apple bobs. "I knew I couldn't try to get you back until I fixed everything."

"You didn't mess up my life, Ben."

"You lost your job."

"And I got a new one, here at the center." I step closer and press my palm to the center of his chest. "And I figured out quite a few things."

"Like what?" He covers my hand with his and gently moves it to his left pec. I can feel the loud *thump-thump* of his heartbeat, and it brings a smile to my lips knowing his heart is pounding as hard as mine.

"I figured out it's okay to allow a few complications into my life, because sometimes complicated is better than being alone. Being lonely."

"You're lonely?"

"Ever since you left," I confess. "And I don't mean lonely in the sense that just anyone'll do. I'm lonely for *you*. I missed you, Ben."

He reaches down and encircles my waist. "I missed you too, Red."

"Really?"

"Yeah. So fucking much."

And then he covers my mouth with a crushing kiss, one of his trademark rough and greedy kisses that leaves me absolutely breathless. I twine my arms around his neck and push my tongue into his mouth, wanting more, needing more.

It's Ben who finally breaks the kiss, groaning softly in my ear as his obvious erection pokes against my navel. "We should stop," he mutters, his warm breath fanning over my forehead. "Anybody could walk in right now."

"Then let's go somewhere private. I'm sure the Lester Hotel has a few rooms available," I tease.

He flashes his movie-star grin. "Maybe later. First we need to get a few things straight."

"I should've known you'd get all demanding on me."

"I'm making it clear, right here and right now, that I'm not leaving you ever again," he says in a stern voice. "If you don't like it, tough."

"I like it," I assure him, fighting a smile. "I'm not going anywhere, either."

"Even when the press gets in our faces again?" His cobalt eyes cloud over. "And I do mean *when*, babe. If we're together, you'll need to get used to the vultures."

"If being with you means getting my picture taken every now and then, it's a sacrifice I'm willing to make." I quirk one eyebrow up. "Like I said, I'm not going anywhere."

He tosses out another hurdle. "Even if I force you to take some time off work and join me in Prague when shooting starts for Alan Goodrich's latest film?"

I gasp. "He gave you a role?"

"Yep. With lines and everything, not just car chases."

"Oh my God, that's amazing!" My eyes light up. "I've never been to Prague."

"Well, you can't stay too long," he warns. "My mom is anxious to start all the wedding plans."

I gape at him. "I'm sorry. Did you say wedding plans?"

"Well, yeah." He grins sheepishly. "I forgot, we're getting married someday. Like maybe in a year? I'll let you pick the date."

I snort loudly. "How kind of you."

His hands slide down my spine to squeeze my ass. "Are you saying you don't want to marry me?"

"Is this seriously a proposal?" I demand.

Ben's blue eyes twinkle. "Nah...it's more of an I love you, and that I see us in this for the long haul."

My heart skips a beat. "I see that too."

"And?"

I meet his expectant gaze. "And what?"

"What else?"

"What do you mean, what else?"

"I just told you I love you!" he sputters. "You're really just gonna leave me hanging like that?"

"Oh. Right." I glide one hand down his back and give his butt a squeeze of my own. "I love you, too."

He chuckles before bringing his lips close to mine. "Of course you do. I'm Ben Barrett, remember?"

The End

Have you read Elle's latest series? Read on for a short preview of
The Chase, the first book in the Briar U saga!

THE CHASE

FITZ

"Dance with me?"

I want to say no.

But I also want to say yes.

I call this the Summer Dilemma—the frustrating, polar reactions this green-eyed, golden-haired goddess sparks in me.

Fuck yes and *hell no*.

Get naked with her. Run far, far away from her.

"Thanks, but I don't like to dance." I'm not lying. Dancing's the worst.

Besides, when it comes to Summer Di Laurentis, my flight instinct always wins out.

"You're no fun, Fitzy." She makes a tsking noise, drawing my gaze to her lips. Full, pink, and glossy, with a tiny mole above the left side of her mouth.

It's an extremely hot mouth.

Hell, everything about Summer is hot. She's hands down the best-looking girl in the bar, and every dude in our vicinity is either staring enviously or glowering at me for being with her.

Not that I'm *with* her. We're not together. I'm just standing next to her, with two feet of space between us. Which Summer keeps trying to bridge by leaning closer to me.

In her defense, she practically has to scream in my ear for me to hear her over the electronic dance music blasting through the room. I hate EDM, and I don't like these kinds of bars, the ones with a dance floor and deafening music. Why the subterfuge? Just call your establishment a nightclub, if that's what you want it to be. The owner of Gunner's Pub should've called this place Gunner's Club. Then I could've turned right around when I saw the sign and spared myself the shattered eardrums.

Not for the first time tonight, I curse my friends for dragging me to Brooklyn for New Year's Eve. I'd way rather be at home, drinking a beer or two and watching the ball drop on TV. I'm low-key like that.

"You know, they warned me you were a curmudgeon, but I didn't believe it until now."

"Who's *they*?" I ask suspiciously. "And hey, wait. I'm not a curmudgeon."

"Hmmm, you're right—the term is kind of dated. Let's go with Groucho."

"Let's not."

"No-Fun Police? Is that better?" Her expression is pure innocence. "Seriously, Fitz, what do you have against fun?"

An unwitting smile breaks free. "Got nothing against fun."

"All right. Then what do you have against *me*?" she challenges. "Because every time I try talking to you, you run away."

My smile fades. I shouldn't be surprised that she's calling me out in public. We've had a whopping total of two encounters, but that's plenty of time for me to know she's the type who thrives on drama.

I hate drama.

"Got nothing against you, either." With a shrug, I ease away from the bar, prepared to do what she's just accused me of—run.

A frustrated gleam fills her eyes. They're big and green, the same shade as her older brother Dean's eyes. And Dean's the reason I force myself to stay put. He's a good friend of mine. I can't be a jackass to his sister, both out of respect for him, and for fear of my well-being. I've been on the ice when Dean's gloves come off. He's got a mean right hook.

"I mean it," I say roughly. "I have nothing against you. We're cool."

"What? I didn't hear the last part," she says over the music.

I dip my mouth toward her ear, and I'm surprised that I barely have to bend my neck. She's taller than the average chick, five-nine or ten, and since I'm six-two and used to towering over women, I find this refreshing.

"I said we're cool," I repeat, but I misjudged the distance between my lips and Summer's ear. The two collide, and I feel a shiver run up her frame.

I shiver too, because my mouth is way too close to hers. She smells like heaven, some fascinating combo of flowers and jasmine and vanilla and—sandalwood, maybe? A man could get high on that fragrance. And don't get me started on her dress. White, strapless, short. So short it barely grazes her lower thighs.

God fucking help me.

I quickly straighten up before I do something stupid, like kiss her. Instead, I take a huge gulp of my beer. Only it goes down the wrong pipe, and I start coughing like it's the eighteenth century and I'm a tuberculosis patient.

Smooth move.

"You okay?"

When the coughing fit subsides, I find those green eyes dancing at me. Her lips are curved in a devilish smile. She knows exactly what got me flustered.

"Fine," I croak, just as three very plastered guys lumber up to the bar and bump into Summer.

She stumbles, and the next thing I know there's a gorgeous, sweet-smelling woman in my arms.

She laughs and grabs my hand. "C'mon, let's get out of this crowd before it leaves bruises."

For some reason, I let her lead me away.

We end up at a high table near the railing that separates the bar's main room from the small, shitty dance floor. A quick look around reveals that most of my friends are drunk off their asses.

Mike Hollis, my roommate, is grinding up on a cute brunette who doesn't seem to mind in the slightest. He's the one who insisted we make the drive to Brooklyn instead of staying in the Boston area. He wanted to spend New Year's with his older brother Brody, who disappeared the moment we got here. I guess the girl is Hollis' consolation prize for getting ditched by his brother.

Our other roommate, Hunter, is dancing with three girls. Yup, three. They're all but licking his face off, and I'm pretty sure one has a hand down his pants. Hunter, of course, is loving it.

What a difference a year makes. Last season he was uneasy about all the female attention, said it made him feel a bit sleazy. Now, it appears he's perfectly cool taking advantage of the perks that come with playing hockey for Briar University. And trust me, there're plenty of perks.

Let's get real—athletes are the most fuckable guys on most college campuses. If you're at a football school, chances are there's a line of jersey chasers begging to blow the quarterback. Basketball school? The groupie pool doubles and triples in size when March Madness comes around. And at Briar, with a hockey team that has a dozen Frozen Four championships under its belt and more nationally televised games than any other college in the country? The hockey players are gods.

Except for me, that is. I play hockey, yes. I'm good at it, definitely. But "god" and "jock" and "superstar" are terms I've never been comfortable with. Deep down, I'm a huge nerd. A nerd masquerading as a god.

"Hunter's got game." Summer is studying Hunter's entourage.

The DJ has switched the beats from electronic garbage to Top 40 hits. Blessedly, he's also turned down the volume, probably in anticipation of the nearing countdown. Thirty more minutes and I can make my escape.

"He does," I agree.

"I'm impressed."

"Yeah?"

"Definitely. Greenwich boys are usually secret prudes."

I wonder how she knows Hunter is from Connecticut. I don't think I've seen them exchange more than a few words tonight. Maybe Dean told her? Or maybe—

Or maybe it doesn't frickin' matter how she knows, because if it *did* matter, then that means the weird prickly sensation in my chest is jealousy. And that, frankly, is unacceptable.

Summer does another visual sweep of the crowd and blanches. "Oh my God. Gross." She cups her hands to create a microphone, shouting, "Keep your tongue in your own mouth, Dicky!"

Laughter sputters out of me. No way Dean could've heard her, but I guess he possesses some sort of sibling radar, because he abruptly pries his lips off his girlfriend's. His head swivels in our direction. When he spots Summer, he gives her the finger.

She blows a kiss in return.

"I'm so glad I'm an only child," I remark.

She grins at me. "Naah, you're missing out. Tormenting my brothers is one of my favorite pastimes."

"I've noticed." She calls Dean "Dicky," a childhood nickname that a nicer person would have stopped using years ago.

On the other hand, Dean's nickname for Summer is "Boogers," so maybe she's right to torture him.

"Dicky deserves to be tormented tonight. I can't believe we're partying in *Brooklyn*," she grumbles. "When he said we were ringing in the New Year in the city, I assumed he meant Manhattan—but then he and Allie dragged me to horrible Brooklyn instead. I feel duped."

I snicker. "What's wrong with Brooklyn? Allie's dad lives around here, doesn't he?"

Summer nods. "They're spending the day with him tomorrow. And to answer your question—what *isn't* wrong with Brooklyn? It used to be cool, before it got overrun by hipsters."

"Hipsters still exist? I thought we were done with that nonsense."

"God, no. And don't let anyone tell you otherwise." She mock shudders. "This whole area is still teeming with them."

She says *"them"* as if they're carriers for a gruesome, incurable disease. She might have a point, though—a thorough examination of the crowd reveals a large amount of vintage attire, painfully skinny jeans on men, retro accessories paired with shiny new tech, and lots and lots of beards.

I rub my own beard, wondering if it places me in the hipster camp. I've been rocking the scruff all winter, mostly because it's good insulation from the bitter weather we've been experiencing. Last week we got hit by one of the worst Nor'easters I've ever seen. I almost froze my balls off.

"They're so..." She searches for the right word. "Douchey."

I have to laugh. "Not all of them."

"Most of them," she says. "Like, see that girl over there? With the braids and the bangs? That's a thousand-dollar Prada cardigan she has on—and she's paired it with a five-dollar tank she probably got at the Salvation Army, and those weird tasseled shoes they sell in Chinatown. She's a total fraud."

I furrow my brow. "How do you know the cardigan cost a grand?"

"Because I have the same one in gray. Besides, I can pick Prada out of any lineup."

I don't doubt that. She was probably deposited into a designer onesie the moment she popped out of her mother's womb. Summer and Dean come from a filthy-rich family. Their parents are successful lawyers who were independently wealthy before they got hitched, so now they're like a mega-rich super-duo who could probably buy a small country without even making a dent in their bank account. I stayed at their Manhattan penthouse a couple times, and it was goddamn unreal. They also have a mansion in Greenwich, a beach house, and a bunch of other properties around the globe.

Me, I can barely make the rent on the townhouse I share with two other dudes. We're still on the hunt for a fourth roommate, though, so my share will go down once we fill that empty room.

I'm not gonna lie—the fact that Summer lives in penthouses and owns clothes that cost thousands of dollars is slightly unsettling.

"Anyway, hipsters suck, Fitzy. No thank you. I'd way rather —oooh! I *love* this song! I had backstage passes to her show at The Garden last June and it was *amazing*."

The ADHD is strong with this one, my friend.

I hide a smile as Summer completely drops her death-to-all-hipsters tirade and starts bobbing her head to a Beyoncé song. Her high ponytail swishes wildly.

"Are you sure you don't want to dance?" she pleads.

"Positive."

"You're the worst. I'll be right back."

I blink, and she's no longer beside me. Blink again, and I spot her on the dance floor, arms thrust in the air, ponytail flipping, hips moving to the beat.

I'm not the only one watching her. A sea of covetous eyes ripples in the direction of the beautiful girl in the white dress. Summer either doesn't notice or doesn't care. She dances alone, without an ounce of self-consciousness. She is completely comfortable in her own skin.

"Jesus," Hunter Davenport rasps, coming up to the table. Like most of the men around us, he's staring at Summer with an expression that could only be described as pure hunger.

"Guess she hasn't forgotten any of those old cheerleading moves." Hunter slants another appreciative look in Summer's direction. When he notices my quizzical face, he adds, "She was a cheerleader in high school. Member of the dance team too."

When did he and Summer engage in a conversation long enough for him to learn these tidbits?

The uncomfortable prickling sensation returns, this time traveling up my spine.

It's not jealousy, though.

"Cheerleading and dance, huh?" I ask lightly. "She tell you that?"

"We went to the same prep school," he reveals.

"No shit."

"Yeah. I was a year behind her, but trust me, every hetero guy with a working dick was familiar with Summer Di Laurentis's cheer routines."

I'll bet.

He claps me on the shoulder. "Gonna hit the head and then grab another drink. Want anything?"

"I'm good."

Not sure why, but I'm relieved that Hunter's not around when Summer returns to the table, her cheeks flushed from exertion.

Despite the frigid temperatures outside, she chose not to wear tights or pantyhose, and, as my old man would say, she's got legs for days. Long, smooth, gorgeous legs that would probably look so hot wrapped around my waist. And the white dress sets off her deep, golden tan, giving her a glowing, healthy vibe that's almost hypnotizing.

"So, you're..." I clear my throat. "You're coming to Briar this semester, huh?" I ask, trying to distract myself from her smokin' body.

She gives an enthusiastic nod. "I am!"

"Are you going to miss Providence?" I know she spent her freshman and sophomore years at Brown, plus one semester of junior year, which makes up half her college career. If it were me, I'd hate starting over at a new school.

But Summer shakes her head. "Not really. I wasn't a fan of the town, or the school. I only went there because my parents wanted me to attend an Ivy League and I didn't get into Harvard or Yale, their alma maters." She shrugs. "Did you want to go to Briar?"

"Definitely. I heard phenomenal things about the Fine Arts program. And, obviously, the hockey program is stellar. They offered me a full ride to play, and I get to study something I'm really into, so..." I offer a shrug in return.

"That's so important. Doing what you love, I mean. A lot of people don't have that opportunity."

Curiosity flickers through me. "What do you love to do?"

Her answering grin is self-deprecating. "I'll let you know when I figure it out."

"Come on, there's got to be something you're passionate about."

"Well, I've *been* passionate about stuff—interior design, psychology, ballet, swimming. The problem is, it never sticks. I lose interest quickly. I haven't found a long-term passion yet, I suppose."

Her candidness surprises me a bit. She seems way more down-to-earth tonight compared to our previous encounters.

"I'm thirsty," she announces.

I suppress the urge to roll my eyes, since I'm sure that's code for *go buy me a drink*. Only, it's not. With a naughty smile, she swipes my beer from my hand.

Our fingers brush briefly, and I pretend not to notice the spark of heat that races up my arm. I watch as she wraps her fingers around the Bud Light bottle and takes a long sip.

She's got small hands, delicate fingers. It'd be a challenge to draw them, to capture the intriguing combination of fragility and surety. Her fingernails are short, rounded and have those white French tips or whatever you call 'em, a style that seems way too plain for someone like Summer. I'd expect extra-long talons painted pink or some other pastel.

"You're doing it again." There's accusation in her tone. A bit of aggravation too.

"Doing what?"

"Zoning me out. Curmudgeoning."

"That's not a word."

"Says who?" She takes another sip of beer.

My gaze instantly fixes on her lips.

Dammit, I gotta stop this. She's not my type. The first time I met her, everything about her screamed *sorority girl*. The designer clothes, the waves and waves of blonde hair, a face that could stop traffic.

There's no way I'm her type, either. I have no idea why she's spending New Year's Eve talking to a scruffy, tatted-up goon like me.

"Sorry. I'm not very chatty. Don't take it personally, okay?" I steal my bottle back.

"Okay, I won't. But if you don't feel like talking, at least entertain me in other ways." She plants her hands on her hips. "I propose we make out."

The Chase is available at all retailers now!

ABOUT THE AUTHOR

A *New York Times, USA Today* and *Wall Street Journal* bestselling author, Elle Kennedy grew up in the suburbs of Toronto, Ontario, and holds a BA in English from York University. From an early age, she knew she wanted to be a writer and actively began pursuing that dream when she was a teenager. She loves strong heroines and sexy alpha heroes, and just enough heat and danger to keep things interesting!

Elle loves to hear from her readers. Visit her website www. ellekennedy.com or sign up for her newsletter to receive updates about upcoming books and exclusive excerpts. You can also find her on Facebook (ElleKennedyAuthor), Twitter (@ElleKennedy), or Instagram (@ElleKennedy33).

Lightning Source UK Ltd.
Milton Keynes UK
UKHW021841280521
384560UK00008B/2026